T3-BUK-831

Big Eyes,
Small Windows

Niek Kemps

Big Eyes, Small Windows

Selected Writings

edited by Charles Esche and Gerrie van Noord

Black Dog Publishing Limited

CONTENTS

INTRODUCTION

Writings by artists are some of the most revealing documents in
contemporary art. They offer an account of a way of thinking that
often parallels the artworks, and provides an insight into a particular artistic
milieu. This selection from the writings of Niek Kemps introduces new
aspects of his work to an English speaking audience. It seems particularly
appropriate to publish this work at a time when the demise of the old
ideological positions permits the invention of new ways of thinking about
art and society. Kemps' writing addresses these issues directly, seeking to
provoke a precise attitude and new awareness in the mind of the reader.
Through the interweaving of essays, dialogues, stories and anecdotes he
invites us to rethink some of our accustomed responses to culture.

This project began in 1994 with an invitation to make a solo exhibition in an
old tram factory in Glasgow, Scotland, which had recently begun to establish
itself as an international gallery. The Tramway exhibition in 1996 was a
notable success for its subtle articulation of the large main gallery space
and its extraordinary central work. This latter piece brought together within
a coherent framework of screens and tables, small-scale works which
reflected on the artist's production over the past fifteen years.

For the catalogue, it seemed fitting to develop the methodology of the
exhibition and not restrict ourselves to discussing the work on display.
Niek Kemps' writings follow closely the development of his own artwork
and it quickly became clear that a book of his collected texts, rather than a
catalogue, would be an apposite response.

The relationship between Kemps' sculptural work and the texts is a complex
one. The texts are neither glosses on the artwork nor completely unrelated.
They deal in part with sources and influences, and in part extend the
psychological and metaphorical play of the plastic work into language.
These parallels are most evident when we examine specific characteristics
of the work and their transformations in the texts. For instance, by using
transparent or semi-opaque surfaces that are themselves obscured, Kemps
creates an effect like blind windows opening out onto an unobservable
view. Their consequent reflectivity throws the viewer's image back onto
the surface of the works, acknowledging a personal presence. They invite
the search for an entrance. Literally, in some cases, by wandering round

the object, and conceptually in many others, where the starting point is an attempt to comprehend a visual cacophony of multiple and layered exposures. Once found, however, the entrance does not lead to some revelatory experience. Being on the inside looking out becomes as tantalising as being outside looking for a way in. The complexity multiplies, and the sense of being out of one's depth is unavoidable. The tension between physical and intellectual understanding remains.

In the texts, these impressions of unsuspected density, blind windows and of being left to fend for oneself become a motif that extends across the different genres of prose, dialogue and essay. Some of the texts emerged from lectures and periods of teaching in various academies, others were written specifically for publications or broadcasts, and further work directly in correspondence with his production as a visual artist. Kemps composed many of these latter texts as artist's pages in various Dutch and international publications. The accompanying photographic images are not illustrations of the words, but analogous evidence that should be weighed separately, though in relation to the text. This dialogue between text and image is true throughout the book, where the full page photographs and drawings also need to be seen neither as works in their own right nor as explications of the writings. Instead, they exist as a visual thesaurus in which shades of additional meaning are created in the combination of image and text, or in the narrative of an image sequence.

The strongest impression I have of Kemps' work is of the Glasgow exhibition, which was the initial impetus for this publication. Standing in the empty factory space of Tramway, I walk towards the *House for Something Called Art*, which is a collaboration between Kemps and Lawrence Weiner. The text on the work reads "STANDING OUTSIDE THE HEAT OF THE SUN", but as I approach the sunlight in the gallery fades and the light bouncing off the polyester and glue turns into a radiance emitting from the sculpture. The edges of the shelves on which the glue sits in gelatinous rectangles shine out and I catch myself thinking, in very personal terms, about the potential clarity that might come with proper organisation and structure. To my right, a long green plastic screen divides and allows me access to the boxed collections laid out on long, glue-topped tables. Walking in, I find a collection of photographs laid out in tiny wooden compartments, again ordered but without obvious meaning. Each image is exposed twice or more, the complexity of lines and forms deceiving the eye. There are no foregrounds or backgrounds, just presence—the images full to the brim. The process of looking closely inevitably excludes much of my awareness of the surrounding situation. I have to rely on certain superficial details to identify the subjects of each photograph. Nudity and surgery, breasts and hands all fall into the same category and become meaningless as signifiers. I can find sense only in the process of looking and in the observation of the point where intellectual inquiry breaks down. I am struggling again, though I sense that beyond this point lies something very pertinent to the work—a different set of expectations and possibilities.

The texts that most closely convey this sense of discovery and confusion are the dialogues. The reader is never clear who is speaking, how many are in the conversation, nor to what extent each recognises the statements of the others. Sometimes, it appears as a babble of different tongues, all allowing each other space to speak but deprived of mutual understanding. It is then the reader's task to gather a narrative and create a sense of place or time. In many of these texts, the intention seems to be to place the reader in a position that loosens the hold of convention and familiarity. The weird flow of the conversations disrupts the hard-wired responses to look and think again about a particular aspect of a recognisable world. *Not the Presence of Distance*, the dialogue about New York, turns the towering verticality of the uptown avenues into endless horizontal walkways, in which the sky becomes a swimming pool at the bottom of a short flight of stairs. The view is blocked, so the necessary space for observation and self-reflection, which are so crucial to both the writings and the sculptural work, must be found elsewhere.

There are certain key concepts and phrases which recur throughout the book and may require some further explanation. The panorama is used as both a description of a view and a metaphorical allusion to a place from which one can oversee a situation that, in the artist's terms, includes both spatial and temporal dimensions. The panorama looks both forward and backward, to the front and behind. From such an exalted position it is possible to gain an understanding that goes beyond description. It is exclusively visual in the sense that the details of the observations cannot be verbalised without at the same time being artificially magnified, and the whole not being encapsulated except in experiential terms. The panorama also relates to certain uses that Kemps makes of the writings of Stephen Hawking and other cosmologists. He quotes Hawking's description of the black hole as a place from which 'not even light can escape' as a link with the proposed meaning of panorama. The black hole becomes the position from which one might gain the ultimate view or, more accurately, mental state. To resolve this contradictory statement, Kemps makes use of the unique aspect of the black hole as a body that swallows matter without any apparent consequence. Kemps uses the theories of entropy and the preservation of energy to imagine the emergence of this light, and hence visuality, into another, unseen dimension. A viewer occupying a position where one could observe both entry and destination, might, by analogy, be permitted a new perspective and understanding, either of their own significance or of social and political developments.

Kemps often refers to this space as an 'in-between state', another key phrase. He uses the term to describe a state that exists in the psyche of the viewer rather than in the manifested physicality of a sculpture, or the narrative of a text. The two short extracts below, one analytical, the other more inventive, are as close as we may expect to a verbal definition from the artist himself:

> The real changes never take place at the moment of revolution, because the revolution —through its very longing for change—searches for a form of true harmony, for the ideal image. The real change occurs usually before or just after, when the revolution is not facing outwards, but inwards. When the conversion takes place in the heart of things. [1]

> We're on our way from A to B, not even knowing where A was or B will be. Despite our increasing speed, the coat and fat wallet on the bonnet don't move. Before I get used to this scene, we reach a beautiful green forest cut by a single-track railway. We walk along the tracks, enjoying the silence and tranquillity. It's impossible to get lost in such an environment. I'm just about to tell my fellow travellers how calm the sea looks, when we're caught by a tidal wave....[2]

These quotations reveal the connective tissue behind many of the texts in the book. They both suggest that a sense of purposeful destination is not the key to looking at art or indeed seeking social and political change. Instead they promote the idea of placing oneself in the midst of things, of making associations out of the material that passes and flows, rather like the rhythm of many of the less structured texts. Kemps encourages us to put ourselves in this 'in-between state', it is 'an attitude and an awareness' which the writings intend to uncover in the reader.[3]

Within this lies not only part of the key to understanding the idea of the 'in-between state', but also the related concern of over-visuality and the negative image, which are both central to the concerns of the writings. In his denial of easy access to his work, Kemps suggests that we need to clear ourselves of preconceptions in order to look again at the same scene we have consumed a hundred times.

> They are everywhere, these moments of contemplation. You just have to sniff the air. That familiar view through your bedroom window can suddenly reveal something new. After years of treating it with weary neglect, you can be captivated by a sight you never noticed before. Does it matter that you were so unreceptive? After all, the eventual discovery is reward in itself... hunting also for an indefinable surplus, a point where the source of inspiration and its outcome... lead to new and unforseeable moments....[4]

He sees in the negative image, or the reversal of the immediately identifiable, a way of delaying recognition for that moment of contemplation to occur. In a Western society, in which visual over-stimulation causes us regularly to disconnect our intellectual faculties from the everyday environment, any examination of our ocular responses is rare. "You won't believe your eyes" might have done as a slogan for early cinema, but it is hardly likely to impress a generation brought up on *Independence Day* and *Terminator*. What is required is a more subtle approach, one based on slight alterations to the familiar. Within this book, these techniques are refined by the formal disjunctures of certain descriptive passages or dialogues.

Kemps has no interest in clarifying the stage beyond these moments of contemplation. His interest is in the moment when the potential for change reveals itself in the mind rather than in any solution to the questions that arise. In common with many contemporary artists, he excludes readings from his work that might suggest a social or political programme, believing that the moment artists adopt a dogmatic position they cease to be able to create. For Kemps, a state of mind that looks to encompass conflicting or unconnected possibilities is the key to his work, as he illustrates in a fascinating aside about the fifteenth-century painter Pisanello.

> In art history, Pisanello is still thought of as a Gothic or late medieval painter. Yet, he foresaw that a new period, which we now call the Renaissance, was about to emerge. He had enough distance to oversee both his own era and the one to come, and was capable of using the tools available to both. He made use of perspective, not one kind but different perspectives, appearing alongside and through each other. He even introduced the open window, a device that was to become a characteristic of Renaissance painting, but he closed it off by putting leaves, insects or flowers in front of it. Thus he remained within his own time and allowed the viewers themselves to anticipate what might come. I think I am looking for something similar in my own work, perhaps at a time not unlike Pisanello's.[5]

The obscured view through the window is a clear reflection of Kemps' own blocked transparency, as is his attribution to Pisanello of the 'in-between state', able to see both the medieval and Renaissance worlds. It suggests that our own post-modern times are not so unlike the fifteenth century, as well as being symptomatic of his creative manipulation of the work of others. Indeed, careful reading might reveal influences other than those directly quoted, particularly from writers such as Don DeLillo, or John Berger. The interest is in the way Kemps identifies aspects of their production that illuminate specific concerns within his own work. For instance, another key term, the 'indefinable surplus' can be found in some measure in both Berger and DeLillo. Its reference to the creation of a sum greater than the component parts of a work is apparent in Berger's writing, especially its simple descriptions of mundane life in southern France.

While the panorama and the surplus are invested with multiple readings and possible attributes throughout the texts, three key essays define a very precise relationship between Kemps' works and research and professional practice outside art. *Art and Consciousness*, *Les Privilèges de la Promenade II*

and *The White Hole* describe the possible conditions in which art can open
up dialogues with science, the natural world and architecture respectively.
Kemps' interest in science stems from his interrogation of the connection
between the intellectual, the emotional and the visual. For him, the scientist
Daniel C. Dennett provides a rational scientific explanation for a phenomenon
that is transparently obvious to the artist. Without the complex process of
discrimination and identification that visual stimuli excite in the brain, the
practice of art would be impossible. It is the gaps, however, which are the
most interesting aspect of Dennett's theories, creating some form of physical
explanation for the psychological notion of an in-between state and the
possibility of recognising surplus value. Similarly, *Les Privilèges de la Promenade*
discusses the artist's reaction to his visit to the Generalife surrounding the
Alhambra Palace in Granada, Spain. This carefully planned and controlled
example of natural and human synergy is described as natural architecture,
with defined spaces for activities that serve the purpose of the garden while
creating routes of engagement for the visitors. By extension, it provides a
justification for art on its own terms and a social reason for its presentation
to an audience

The third key essay, *The White Hole*, provides a tour of the decaying
monuments to the industrial era. In a style, which flirts with nostalgia,
Kemps analyses the changing aesthetic of the factory building from its
outset as a mimetic copy of an aristocratic country house to the functionalist
sheds of the industrial estate. In the essay, industry itself appears as though
in an in-between state, where the relics of a past industrialism are neither fully
productive nor yet consigned to touristic stasis. Here there is a significant
potential for art to create new meaning out of the old. To mention briefly
another influential artist for Kemps, Robert Smithson's ideas of the non-site
are here expounded within a European context, and with the conceptual
model of the circle replacing the spiral.

In many ways, *Big Eyes, Small Windows* serves as an antidote to the
populism that seems to hold sway over large areas of contemporary art
presentation and museology today. Through the texts, we find an artist
who stands in contrast both to this current *fin-de-siècle* atmosphere and its
desire for simplicity or accessibility. Niek Kemps gives us all the
complexity and trusts us, as we should be trusted, to have the will and
intelligence to hold it in our own minds.

CHARLES ESCHE

Notes

1. Art and Consciousness, p. 27.
2. The Jet Blast Cooling Pump II, p. 93.
3. From an unpublished conversation with the artist in Wenduine, Belgium, in August 1997.
4. Sunken Fence, p. 23.
5. See note 3.

CTION. PASSAGES. BIBLIOGRAPHY. NOTES AND VARIATIONS.

THE FORUM ROMANUM IN ROME
THE PYRAMIDS OF GIZEH

THE TOWN HALL IN BASEL
THE KASBA IN MARRAKESH
SAN MARCO SQUARE IN VENICE
THE CATHEDRAL OF SANTIAGO DE COMPOSTELA
THE GOLDEN GATE BRIDGE IN SAN FRANCISCO
SANSSOUCI PALACE IN POTSDAM
THE KREMLIN IN MOSCOW

HAMPTON COURT NEAR LONDON
THE MAUSOLEUM IN ANGKOR WAT

SUNKEN FENCE

WE CROSSED A BRIDGE.
    On reaching the other side
we glanced down to see a small
paddock far below.
Not an official paddock, but a
piece of no-man's land,
surrounded by highways.
The daughter of a local
councillor had confiscated
the land some time ago to
train her horse.
I don't know if it was the
vertiginous view, the banality of
the surroundings, their
emptiness or the pleasure of
the company, but I can't shake
this image out of my mind.
I keep imagining what the
daughter and her horse look
like, playing out scenarios from
a film that doesn't exist.
It stays with me for some
reason, the incongruous sight
of a well-tended paddock in
the midst of speeding
commuter traffic.
It would be pointless to add
anything or attempt some kind
of visual analogy.
The source of inspiration and
its potential outcome seem
to have merged, it's as simple
as that.

Time vanishes.
Past and future meet in this
one image, a restless image
that plays in the mind like a
moving panorama.
For a moment I am set free
from the constant flow of
interwoven images, my
senses already filled by this
singular vision.
They are everywhere, these
moments of contemplation.
You just have to sniff the air.
That familiar view through
your bedroom window can
suddenly reveal something new.
After years of treating it with
weary neglect you can be
captivated by a sight you never
noticed before.
Does it matter that you were so
unreceptive? After all, the
eventual discovery is a reward
in itself.
Perhaps here is something
which touches on the value of
artists. Could they be thought
of as detectives searching for
such unacknowledged
moments, forgotten scents and
neglected atmospheres?
Looking for the extraordinary
in the banal?
And, perhaps, also hunting
for an indefinable surplus, a
point where the source of
inspiration and its outcome
not only merge but lead to
new and unforeseeable
moments like this.

ART AND CONSCIOUSNESS:
IDENTICAL TWINS

Having secrets is an essential part of being human. Secrets play a big role in the use of language. A secret is something I know that you don't know, but also something I know that you don't know I know — it gives me control.

Daniel C. Dennett

AN UNUSUAL SERIES OF PROGRAMMES was shown on Dutch television recently. Six scientists—men at the top of their profession—were brought together in a round-table discussion. Probably the hope was that this meeting would produce 'great thoughts', possibly a historic moment or two.

Before the final discussion, the interviewer visited the six scientists and talked to them about themselves, their work, their experiments, their dreams. The result was a series of six engaging programmes, lasting an hour and a half each. The interviewer asked each of his interviewees what they thought about the other five and these disclosures opened each of the individual programmes. A short introduction followed by the interview itself. Only the face of the interviewee filled the screen, a refreshing change from the usual superficiality and hectic pace of television.

I found the interview with Daniel Dennett completely compelling, probably because I discovered so many similarities with my own way of thinking and because his starting points lie close to those of art. I also found it absorbing to see what the other scientists had to say about him. As with artists they argued amongst themselves, disagreeing about the fundamentals.

Rupert Sheldrake:

> Dennett's very clever and I appreciate the quickness of his mind but his starting points are all wrong. He's starting from a materialist point of view, trying to fit the mind into some kind of computing-machine model—it's curiously old-fashioned.

Oliver Sacks:

> I think it'll be very interesting to meet him—he is so concerned with higher mental functions and consciousness. I think he may come over as the most philosophical member of our group. But I wonder if there will be any point of agreement or reconciliation between us.

Stephen J. Gould:

> A colleague of mine at university… much too committed to strict Darwinian interpretation. [laughing] Somehow we've got to broaden him out to understand how rich evolutionary theory is. But he has very interesting things to say about intelligence and consciousness.

Freeman Dyson:

> He's a philosopher so maybe I'd like to ask him: does science make a difference to you? Is it important for you to know whether the universe is finite or infinite? As a philosopher, is that the kind of question you want to know the answer to?

Stephen Toulmin:

> Dennett… does seem to be the brightest and in some ways the most interesting of the people who are still stuck in the old groove. I mean, this whole cognitive science trait seems to me to be one more theoretical artefact we don't need. And I don't think it focuses on the problems of the mind in a way that is going to make them any more soluble in the long run. It's just going to keep people in the business of trying to reconcile our understanding of psychology with an out-of-date view of physics.

In the round-table discussion that concluded the series, the interviewer confronted several of the scientists with their remarks. It was striking that they all partially withdrew their comments and conceded the strength of Dennett's case. So which opinion was relevant? Which comment had lasting value? Is the first one, made when the person was not present, sharper and more radical and the judgment given in the general discussion more subtle? How do you come to a precise definition?

This is what fascinates me. In sculpture, it is not so much the formal, technical aspects in which I am interested, nor even the viewer's emotional response. What delights me is a certain precision of thought, the assumption of a position and the fundamental, singular imperative that permits you to make it manifest.

> Terror is a transitional phase. Iconoclasm is outward looking—never facing inwards. But there is no point in demolishing. The real changes never take place at the moment of revolution, because the revolution—through its very longing for change— searches for a form of true harmony, for the ideal image. The real change occurs usually before or just after, when the revolution is not facing outwards, but inwards. When the conversion takes place in the heart of things. Therefore there is no point in making art that uses the existing language in these times—it is simply no longer viable, you can't use the same words or the traditional system of the picture.

> Yet the circle is not complete—you can't deny that people still make things. You shouldn't have to place yourself outside art—you should arm yourself with the knowledge of all the art that has been made. The artist takes up reality, responds to it and reflects it back on itself. But that is nothing more than the result of perception. By allowing the observation to take place and using it together with a knowledge of art, you have the exact point from which you can respond to art.

I wrote that in 1982, eleven years ago. Am I mistaken—or has nothing changed? Is this statement still valid? Or should it be more precise—more adapted to today's world?

Dennett says:

> Not all information enters the brain at one point. Once perceptions, sounds or words enter through the eyes or ears they are interpreted by specialist parts of the brain. The parts that interpret words are different from the parts that interpret music or other sounds. And in all probability, while you listen to words, you also start to form a mental image, even though you are looking at me. For example, if I start to tell you about a theatre, you immediately form a quasi-visual picture of a theatre that you know, the seats, the stage and so forth. While you listen, your brain is busy in all sorts of ways, trying to understand my words. And the result is that you forget the words but remember what they were about. It's happening already—you couldn't repeat word for word what I've just said. But you've got the gist of it. The actual information has already vanished forever.

I often imagine what it would be like to suddenly become blind. I imagine it would be possible to recall all the images I've seen through the years and stored in my memory, so that being an artist would not have to stop. We all have a bookcase full of books. But how many of them have we read—really read? A similar kind of fantasy is to shut yourself off from the world with only this bookcase full of books. You'd have enough to last a lifetime.

But Dennett kills my dream.

> Instead of information, something that is stored for a longer time in a number of places takes its place. The memory is distributed somehow in the brain. Memory is not like taking a can off the shelf, opening it and tipping out its contents. It is always a process of re-interpretation. Even when you relive something very powerfully and with all the vivid details, it is not like watching a movie. Time has been twisted round and only the essence remains.

Emmenthal consciousness.

We are astonished when we notice the huge gaps in our consciousness, holes in space and time, like a huge blind spot in our eyes, big enough to hide six full moons, piled one on top of the other. You usually don't notice these gaps, because you don't know what you're missing.

I find this extremely satisfying—a work of art not like a unified whole but burst into bits like the shrapnel of a grenade. Innumerable gaps and blind spots which we can certainly try to find but which—especially in the first instance—don't reveal themselves. Precision is never linear, not like a story that fits hand-in-glove. Precision, which I believe to be necessary at present, can be found between words and between things.

How carefully do people look? Listen? Use their senses?

Is it really necessary to take in everything at one glance, immediately, in order to understand and interpret it. Is not the concept of precision much more relevant to the formulation of a question, than the provision of a well-considered statement?

Dennett:

> It's the same with consciousness. What matters is what you think there is. We think there are no gaps in our consciousness. We ignore the gaps and because we ignore them, their existence is not important. That is also why it's so difficult to demonstrate that they're there. But there are ways to call up the gaps and see the blind spot. In order to do so you have to see the edge. To see the edge you require receptors on both sides of the gap. But on the inside there are no receptors, so you can't see it. In fact you can only see your blind spot by letting something disappear into it while you're watching. That's quite easy to do. You put two crosses on a wall. You shut one eye. You look at one of the crosses and move your head towards it until at a given moment you can't see the other cross. It has disappeared into the blind spot. There are other gaps like this.

Six people sitting round a table. Only politely interested to begin with. They are superficially in agreement but soon differences start to fly back and forth. How should precision be defined? Agreement, conflicts of opinion or the confrontation itself?

'Sculpture' is an obsolete term from a time when art was still subdivided on the basis of material. However, such subdivision is no longer possible. Nowadays art tends to be labelled according to 'movement', 'period' or a way of thinking. A work of art consists of various elements that together form a particular piece. Artists take a position in relation to each of the different elements. They reflect, then choose materials, forms and colours. They decide on a measurement, a scale, smooth or rough, dark or light, complex or simple. Artists ponder over presentation, over light, contrast and resemblance. They take a position, but one which is always influenced by culture and time. Indeed, the artist reacts to them. I think this reaction should be as radical as possible. This radicality serves the idea but is not subservient to it. There are many works that attempt to do this and are possibly even radical, but I wouldn't immediately call them works of art.

I find the word image an impossible one. We use it as if it referred to a unity—an object you can look at. It seems as if we continually need to simplify and to see one thing where there are many. The brain has at least 32 centres for visual information alone. So any image we see is almost automatically divided into 32 different aspects in order to be stored. It is as if anything you look at shatters at the moment of reception and is later assembled, like parts of a mosaic, to form a whole. What we call an image is in fact the result of a negotiated process between these 32 visual sections, not to mention the countless other parts that deal with other organs of perception.
The whole communication system that links all aspects—that combines, reduces or deduces—is responsible for creating something that we can call a complete image, but is only the sum of a series of negotiations.

Emmenthal consciousness once more.

Are these blind spots in our consciousness more fundamental, showing moments of insight that go deeper than merely wanton forgetfulness? Is Dennett's secret actually a blind spot? Why is it that having acquired a certain basic store of knowledge, the desire to know gradually gives way to a state of not wanting to know? Is the blind spot not infinitely more interesting than all the so-called images we can see?

A work of art is not a centre. It is a receptor, set on the border of the blind spot and only visible for those who really concentrate upon it. But how do you define what is there? Everyone I ask will say that he or she sees a work of art but I don't think that is the case.

It requires precision in the definition of what you see and prefer not to see.

It requires another language with different metaphors.

It requires a different way of listening.

All the senses have to be used in another way—you must read between words, look between things, feel between senses.

Take twenty young artists from different countries with different back-grounds, put them together and within a very short time a small number of them will find a certain level of agreement. At roughly the same moment, the others will no longer be taken seriously. They won't be included in the important moments, in the times between the formalities.

I have gradually become less interested in the radical statement, the uncompromising remark or in sculpture as an autonomous given. I adopt a position in between.

Between things, between time, between precision (a linguistic impossibility).

It results in the inability to define, to name things—with the unpleasant consequence that in the end you can't talk about anything. You can't see anything. It's just there. Born out of a sense of necessity.

You have landed in a blind spot, in a gap in your consciousness.
Art and consciousness, non-identical twins.

IN

"The difference between the present, and what
memory imposes on us, appeals to me."
"Do you mean that memories seriously affect
our ability to judge?"
"Or that the character of a judgement is based
on the difference between past and present?"
"I wouldn't go that far."
"The present is so diffuse, it's all too tempting
to fall back on the past to get a grip."
"That sounds a bit clichéd."
"No, it's more a case of despair."
"Is the present really as diffuse as you suggest?
I don't think so. Actually, the present—the here
and now—is constantly moving, a light-
hearted Spacewalk."
"It's only diffuse if you don't take part."
"Those on the Spacewalk understand the joy
and fun of moving."
"Do you have any statistics?"
"No, but few let go. Many ignore the past,
even more use it to avoid facing the present."
"That's a bit vague."
"I'll give you an example: every day readers
separate themselves from the real world with a
newspaper. They seem up-to-date, but in fact
they have no concept of the present. Floating
in a timeless dimension that we know as reality."

"A two-month-old newspaper is just as
interesting as tomorrow's."
"Exactly."
"So is the result that the reader no longer notices
the various misrepresentations?"
"Then becomes entangled?"
"It's easier to consume experience and knowledge
than to digest it, something can easily be
labelled 'new'."
"One experience forgotten even before you've
started the next."
"Apparently everyone has an opinion, everyone
informed, everyone a critic."
"The law of mediocrity."
"All equal, all the same."

TE

"The world has never been so dense."
"What did you say? Dense?"
"All the same, everything full, everywhere."
"Are you referring to the way Western civilisation
has penetrated even the smallest village in
the jungle?"
"No. I mean the confusing way events rapidly
succeed one another, leaving everything diffuse
and complex."
"The centre of multiplicity—completely different
events, occurring within a very short span
of time?"
"Not in so many words. I mean the impossibility
of disentangling events, without any sense
of precision."
"Like a bad call by a referee, played back in
slow-mo, for all to see?"
"Exactly."
"So is this about the impotence of analysis?"
"And its consequences—everything is brought
back into line."
"On the sole basis of form, or content as well?"
"It starts with form, but I wouldn't be surprised
if—eventually—differences in content will fade
as well."
"Liberating us from the urge to stand out, or
will there be a fly in the ointment? Not everyone
is a fan of conformity."
"That's a tough one. Most original ideas are
usually appropriated."
"Resulting in instant accessibility."
"However, I do believe that it's intrinsically human
to want to compare on the basis of quality."
"True enough, but it's pretty difficult to spot
quality, when everyone tows the same line."
"The law of mediocrity?"
"Afraid so."
"All the same, all equal."

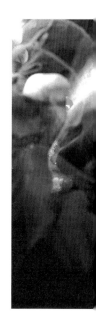

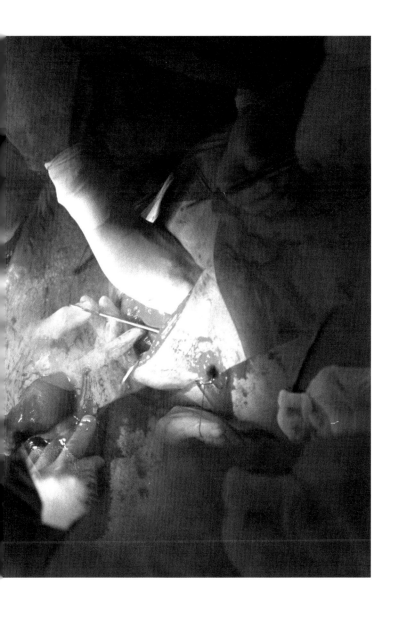

"Can the process of bringing everything into line be stopped?"
"I think so. Change—in every sense of the word—begins here."
"I trust you're not referring to distinguishing on the basis of a simple contrast?"
"No, no, no. Although it's amusing to see people bending over backwards."
"Looking for what we all need, but aren't even aware of?"
"The niche in the market."
"Mass-production versus the hand-made, black against white, square against circle."
"Except that with the first example things are more complex. The hand-made is a recurring theme. It's generally connected to authenticity."
"The hand-made as the only genuine article?"
"Back to basics. A return to the rural. Getting your hands dirty."
"Once again the artist in search of the primitive."
"Yes, using his bare hands to depict the basic essence of mankind for the umpteenth time."
"That's not only redundant, that's an over-simplification."
"Don't get me wrong. Physicality is legitimate, provided that one is aware of the past."
"So, are the concepts 'hand-made', 'authenticity', and 'human body' the same?"
"No, you have to be more specific. Hand-made is too often a contrived attempt to look authentic. Authenticity is necessary, and the human body is a subject, nothing more."
"So, does this confusion come from associating the manual with the authentic?"
"That's what I think. Having said that—what's left of the concept of authenticity?"
"The confusion comes from the fear of the modern?"
"It wouldn't make any difference if everyone were a modernist."
"In other words, towing the line."
"All equal, all the same."

AL

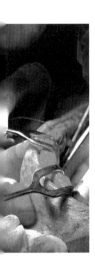

"Bringing everything into line comes from our
urge to stand out."
"Does this need stem from the desire for
real change?"
"Unfortunately not. Standing out is simply a
matter of rejecting the past."
"All you have to do is shift your direction, and
you're different?"
"A vicious circle. Round, and around, and around,
and around..."
"Like a dog chasing its tail."
"Grey is taboo, geometry has been and gone,
mass-production back to the hand-made."
"The hand-made seems to be a recurring theme."
"Obviously."
"A different skill, only because of its
individual nature."
"So, the individual signature doesn't guarantee
any distinction at all?"
"That's right. You can't stick your head
in the sand."
"As if Michelangelo never existed."
"Or Courbet, or Broodthaers."
"Yeah, but I still see the human touch as a source
of inspiration."
"Granted. It can still be interesting, but only if
you acknowledge the past and the present."
"Why so cynical?"
"There's a difference between the action of
the individual artist and the physical touch
as a source."
"Don't you ever get bored with the expression of
the individual, negating history?"
"That type is nothing more than an obvious
attempt to appear authentic."
"Whereas the principle of personal expression
plays up to the all consuming quest to discover
'the genius'."
"Alone, locked in his attic, safe from
the art world."
"Guaranteeing authenticity?"
"Well, it's a simple, naive attempt at
being unique."
"The result?"
"All the same, all equal."

PRECISELY

The streets are remarkably quiet. Somewhere in the distance the sound of a radio, the voice of a football commentator covering an important match.

How still it is.

For once we can walk, undisturbed. Not much is said. It's been a long time since we could enjoy such serene silence. The colour of the buildings seems fresher, the stench of the streets less pungent. As long as both teams are trying to win rather than avoiding defeat, peace will reign.

I've never really understood why people in the arts still think in terms of factions—critics, the opponents of artists? Maybe I am too lenient.

Critics maintain a difficult position; sandwiched between artworks, artists and the public.

A comfortable position, if only they didn't want to belong.

It's no joke trying to decipher the sometimes incomprehensible whims of an artist in a way that informs the public without aggravating the artist in question.

And, to top it all, their articles may never be read.

I've never been a fan of dogmas—preachers and pharmacists waving their fingers in the air, explaining the world, imposing their laws.

I'd rather go against the grain. It's not that I don't like sweeping statements, I just prefer them coming at me in hundreds. Nicely mixed—like scrambled proverbs.

Most of the time I am my own critic.

When a work is finished, I invite the occasional visitor to my studio. It's my way of introducing the work to the outside world. Whatever they say about my work, I consider it to be neither presumptuous nor shocking.

I love watching people getting all worked up trying to interpret a work, like a relentless attempt to crack the secret or solve a problem. Who cares?

There is the interpretation of the viewers, and there is the artist's kitchen —the background, the climate or the mood out of which the artwork grew.

I like to keep my distance.

Singularity, not to be confused with simplicity, is something I despise. The desire to clarify the world leads to the singular. Complexity creates the possibility for various layers to exist concurrently, blending into an unknown whole.

Let me be clear: complexity is not mystery. Mystery, or mystification, is an age-old trick to make something look more interesting and more important than it actually is.
It might be tempting to create an aura around you, with obscure and convoluted phrases and quotes; in fact it's no more than an easy way out.

When work leaves a studio, the public can do with it what it wants. A work of art should be open to interpretation—in every sense of the word. It should radiate the patina that it acquired when it was created.
Most people seem to forget that when a work is first presented in a gallery or museum, where it is scrutinised, discussed and reviewed, it has already been completed—long ago. It is a finished chapter, a closed book.
The viewer's response is not that important to me. I only bother stepping in if his reaction is one-dimensional, or when it comes to a critic hiding behind clichés that negate the complexity of the work in question.
Complexity requires precision.

People are back out on the streets again.
Crowds are shouting, celebrating, waving their flags victoriously.
Meanwhile the losers sneak away silently.
So much for peace and quiet.

"This town is new to me."

"How do you like it?"

"The steam oozing up from of the streets is quite an impressive sight."

"It's like the sidewalk is the top level of some kind of weird life-support machine."

"It's a bit dated, though."

"What do you mean?"

"It reminds me of those steam-engines from a hundred years ago."

"Their sluggish pace seems a far cry from what the city promises today."

"Dinky Toys flashing by, people falling over themselves in a rush?"

"Not to mention the buildings soaring up into the sky."

"This is just about the most horizontal city I have ever seen."

"But what about all those skyscrapers?"

"Once you get between them you lose sight of the overall picture."

"You mean the streets are like tunnels and the skyscrapers break up the sky."

"Don't you see it's because the view is blocked that the skyscrapers keel over. You feel as though you're standing on a short flight of steps, looking out over a vast blue swimming pool."

"A pool you could walk right across."

"Two roofs, no horizon."

"The buildings are high but look flat; the ground appears solid but is transparent."

"Besides, you wouldn't feel safe if all that imposing verticality were really there."

"You always have a good time in the back of a limo with the TV on and a glass full of champagne."

U.

"The eagle's so close, I can almost touch it."
"It looks as if the helicopters are below us, but then again..."
"Aren't you two exaggerating?"
"Look around you. The clouds are as soft as pillows."
"Yeah... that's quite a feeling!"
"What kind of feeling?"
"I have to say this is a spectacular view."
"Stunning."
"It's as though height has transformed into the shimmering surface of a pool."
"What strikes me the most is that there hardly seems to be any difference between the old and the modern."
"Of course. From up here all kinds of styles sit side by side."
"Look how modern the past appears."
"The higher you go, the older it gets."
"The buildings are merging below us."
"In spite of the huge differences, everything looks flat."
"So there's no view left?"
"Precisely, the view has become a postcard."
"A live transmission."
"Complete with atmospheric interference."
"Are you telling me that there's no more view, height, old or modern?"
"Isn't that a little over the top?"
"Sorry, I got carried away for a moment."
"Anyway, I won't give up. Romantic dreams and nostalgic speculations are over and done with."
"The death of the view."
"The world flat, again."
"And the helicopters below."
"What about the eagle?"

L.

"Nothing can beat these cabins for luxury."
"Give me brightly coloured plastic seats and a whiff of excitement any day."
"The view is much better from here."
"Behind the glass, safe and sound."
"Defined in every detail."
"Excuse me?"
"The live event has been replaced by an immense screen. We're meant to watch the event but at the same time we can see every drop of sweat. What actually happens is almost irrelevant."
"A little man disappearing into the distance."
"Literally and..."
"Even the brass band is in full stereo."
"The detail has overcome the panorama."
"Today, images of the world consist only of a succession of details. Images, even multiple ones, seem to be selected without any coherent reason."
"A topsy-turvy world."
"A celebration of the baroque."
"And those huge screens complete the celebration?"

"Well, they do muddle the concepts of 'here' and 'there'."
"I have to admit that it is still possible to distinguish between the two, but I can well imagine that changing too."
"It's true that you can no longer tell the difference between what you see and what actually happens."
"Just imagine the same thing happening to the details—a cheerful world from which reality has been expelled."
"That would certainly be convenient. You'd never have to move, yet you'd still be in control of everything."
"Modern day voyeurism."
"Exactly."
"Man extracted from reality, to become part of an eternal fiction."
"I can't wait."

G.

"The sky's the limit."
"Because it's so clear today?"
"No. The other day I saw something on TV that really fascinated me."
"What was it?"
"Calgary. The most sophisticated techniques, aerodynamic design, ultra-modern electronics. The image of top international sport today."
"Endless training, all scientifically monitored. The ultimate performance."
"The athlete as machine, trained by sensitive computers."
"1.09.14 seconds. The runner-up 0.0001 seconds behind."
"The one thing they can't measure is the pressure of competition, the stress of public scrutiny."
"Perhaps they'll get around to that one day."

"All these intricate devices mean that today's victories are won by the smallest of margins."
"A last, desperate attempt to distinguish one man from another, when distinction has long proved to be irrelevant."
"Desperation justifies any means."
"Besides, I'm not really interested in discussing ethics."
"The phenomenon itself is what fascinates me."
"Speed?"
"The ultimate speed, the ultimate height."
"Even better, the actual limit."
"A limit suggests an end, but once reached the limit seems to shift time and again."
"The sad thing is we don't live in a world without limits, that would make a lot of things easier."
"I disagree. As our view of the world changes, so do limits. Right now the series of digits after the decimal point is expanding. Research at both ends of the scale—the microscopic and the macroscopic—is pushing the limit ever further."
"Are you saying that there's some artificial link between the parts and the whole, like a marriage of convenience?"
"That's the state of affairs in science. But it's no longer a case of either microscopic detail or universal whole."
"The limit of both those terms seems to have been breached."
"I can almost touch the eagle."

15.9
TAKAMATSOE-ZOEKA, OSAKA

An attack may lack ingenuity, but it must be delivered with supernatural speed.

15.6
THE GRIMALDI CAVES, VENTIMIGLIA

"Go, sir, gallop, and don't forget that the world was made in six days. You can ask me for anything you like, except time."

CASTLE HILL ARCH, FILLEIGH
HALDON BELVEDERE, DODDISCOMBSLEIGH

DRYDEN TOWER, BILSTON
THE ROCKET SHIP, AYSGARTH
RALPH ALLEN'S SHAM CASTLE, BATH
ROMULUS AND REMUS ON THE A39 NEAR WEST HORRINGTON
ROUSHAM EYECATCHER, STEEPLE ASTON
LYVEDEN NEW BIELD, BRIGSTOCK
MCCAIG'S FOLLY, OBAN

THE RENDLESHAM LODGES, BENTWATER
MAD JACK FULLER'S SUGAR CONE, BRIGHTLING PARK

The professor's the
confirmed. It was t
that many a scientis
interference in the
cortex; mnemextirp
for the patient life-
of a small operatio
complex is determ
he cerebral electric
what needs
craniotomie ne
operation req
place a day proc
the operation tabl

(fou

in that respect I think
Let yourself be seduced, but c

(on

ortion was brilliantly
ition of an ideal
haunting. A small
tor, in the cerebral
the destruction of a,
g, memory, by way
ict members of the
brain cells in
etric and in
en away. Nowa
The entire
nd can take
t gets up from
es home, relieved.

nts)

ice to Odysseus is valuable:
re you're sufficiently armed."
he)

INTERIOR

A couple of years ago I went to the Trocadero in Paris. One of its wings is a museum, the name of which now escapes me.

It was as good as empty—scarcely a visitor in sight. The rooms were vast and everything looked a bit shabby. In every other room a guard in blue, usually slumped in his chair, was taking a nap or reading a cheap paperback. The museum displays remnants of decorations and redundant pieces of sculpture that were once installed around Paris. You find countless numbers of maquettes that were once used to convince people of 'Progress'. Now they're here, dumped and dusty, paintless and ragged. Almost devoid of visitors, a huge sense of timelessness, tranquillity at last.

In Montpellier, there is a tiny museum, usually closed. If you want to see it, it is customary to ask the concierge—an archetypal French farmer's wife complete with apron, stirring a big pan of soup. Clutching a huge bunch of keys, she grumpily leads the way. Within the museum there are three little rooms, each containing several cupboards that the concierge unlocks one by one. Once opened, drawings appear displayed behind glass in hinged wooden frames. It turns out to be a wonderful collection, including works by Pisanello and Leonardo da Vinci. I couldn't really look at them properly with the ill-tempered concierge breathing down my neck. After five or six cupboards, you are afraid to ask her to open any more. You can practically hear her say: "Are we done now?"

Art has actually failed to capitalise on the trend that brought it into Joe Public's front room in the last decades. Busloads of visitors hop from exhibition to exhibition. It's impossible to open a mainstream magazine without coming across a page on art. Who says art is elitist? On the contrary, art seems no more than any other welcome addition to the tourist trail. Taking its cue from Ibiza and the Ardêche, you even have a Picasso exhibition at the Makkum Municipal Museum in Friesland. Coach parties welcome, group discounts available, refreshments included.

As a result of this popular interest, even politicians have discovered art. Local councillors are queuing up to cut ribbons. But are these really signs of a more genuine interest in art? I doubt it. Are people actually being educated to develop a wider, deeper interest in culture? Is the general tendency to educate prompted by a sacred belief in art? Or is it nothing more than a game of hide-and-seek, overlooking the real issues that have concerned artists for ages? The simple truth is that it is easy to ignore topics that really matter. It is better as an artist to attract no attention at all, than to attract this half-hearted kind of attention. This doesn't just apply to contemporary art, but to art of all times.

STOP
The sky is blue.
STOP

What we need at the moment are private museums—places that don't force themselves upon the world like some kind of pompous peacock. Instead, we need places that serve as shelters, sites of tranquillity protected from the outside world, only accessible to those genuinely interested.

Let's have a look at the situation in The Hague, at the Hofvijver, the pond by the Binnenhof, the Dutch parliament, in particular.
Is this pond a meeting place?
Not really. If that's what it was meant to be, you should at least be able to walk *around* it. Its sole function at the moment is to mirror the buildings that surround it.
The one spot that could be rehabilitated is the place where horses were once washed and tended to. To become a meeting place you should be able to walk freely around it or build a bridge that crosses it. Then it has the chance to become the Tuileries of The Hague.

Museums

There appears to be an all-encompassing anxiety in The Netherlands to introduce design. It is thought of as an instrument to make things more accessible to a larger public. Buildings and exhibitions are now contracted to designers on a regular basis. The outcome often speaks for itself. What can you say about the presentation of Malevich's Black Square in the Stedelijk Museum in Amsterdam? The designer of the exhibition thought it might be nice to present the painting on a huge concave wall, facing a panel with an explanatory text three times the size of the painting itself.

Even the Mauritshuis in The Hague cannot escape this kind of terror.
It is one of the few publicly accessible stately homes in The Netherlands. Ironically the visitor is forced to enter the museum through the staff entrance, the proverbial back door, denying one the rare chance to experience the grandeur of a stately entrance. Instead, you find yourself in a basement —decorated with pretentious marble and stainless steel—from where only a glimpse of the beautiful hallway can be seen. Whose idea was that? How

about the combination of period rooms and modern lighting? Or, for that matter, the explanatory texts on overbearing pedestals? I despise this type of design and everything that goes with it. These embellishments are absolutely unnecessary, the Mauritshuis is beautiful in itself.

The other local museums suffer from the same abuse. Everything in this country is neatly painted, brightly polished and as spotless as can be. Design has infested the entire cultural machine.
Nobody is to blame personally, though it is clear that it is a problem particular to the Dutch. Beyond our borders you are far less likely to encounter this kind of terror in the name of culture.
Therefore I suggest sacking all designers, and don't bother calling in the decorators for another year or so either. Have a party.

Adventure

Adventure surpasses the dream, because the dream is actually nothing but a desired cliché. Adventure avoids clichés and is prepared for unpleasant experiences.

What is the chance of having an adventure on the banks of the Hofvijver? It could only happen if mass tourism was banned and the individual granted total privilege. Only then could the Hofvijver serve not only as a washing place (very public), or a meeting point (nice and cosy), but also as a series of spaces allowing for individual experiences. Art can prompt these experiences. Hence the artist has to be inspired, not just by the umpteenth public commission—the equestrian monument is beautiful and serves its purpose. This is the place to articulate what is already there in those rows of stately homes. Allow some of them, the ones that are sometimes unoccupied for months, to be used by artists, theatre directors or filmmakers and allow the lone visitor to come in and watch. He may be followed by a person looking for a new office in the same building, but that doesn't matter. It may give the businessman a new idea or two. Even the estate agent might get something out of it.

Just remember—one visitor at a time.

That could be the ambition of this project, to create an atmosphere similar to the one in Montpellier or the Paris Trocadero. Bring in the sleepy guard and the short-tempered custodian. Tempt people into their own private playground.

WONDERLAND JUNGLE I

dreams, matches, grass seed, Polder taxes, Delft, parking lot

"Could you eat a six-course meal?"
"That depends on the quality and the quantity of each course."
"The wine list looks terrific."
"If you're really convinced that you're right and someone can prove you wrong, you're usually tempted to go along with that person's theory."
"Theory or Person?"
"If someone demonstrates that your theory is flawed, it doesn't necessarily mean that his is right. That is what you suggested before."
"I don't quite remember..."
"You were beside yourself, because he dismissed everything you said. That doesn't mean that he was right."
"He?"
"Just don't take what he said to heart."
"Memory isn't linear: it's based on true experiences, as well as open to hypothetical experiences."
"A glass of Chardonnay?"
"Yeah, that's allowed."
"Let me put it differently. You do something that results in A. You adopt a certain theory that explains that A is the result of your actions."
"What did I order last time?"
"A mixed marriage, between a wood pigeon and a quail?"
"I do understand, when you refer to the past essentially determining the way you experience things now, the way you hear or read."
"Being overly verbose will get you nowhere."
"This has to be science."
"I've got a knack for both science and humanities."
"Good for you."
"Some more wine, please."

"Alright, I accept that the concept of the image
has lost its meaning. Photographs are no longer
accepted as the ultimate proof, all images can
be manipulated."

"Take a collection of photographs of towers.
They can easily be assembled by
computer programmes."

"Of course."

"It's simple. Our overly-visual society will
eventually reject the image. Perhaps a bit odd,
since the world will still exist as images."

"It seems contradictory: the image loses its
meaning, yet will continue to exist, albeit with a
different value."

"Suppose you accept that condition, would it be
negative or positive?"

"I'd have to say it would be a wonderful chaos."

"I love it, it has cheered me up tremendously."

"But wouldn't it lead to the world falling apart?"

"Not necessarily."

"Your thinking is too one-dimensional. You
disregard our potential as human beings."

"For most people, the visual is a million times
easier to grasp than text."

"Really?"

"One single image says more than three pages of
text ever will. That will never change. What will
change is that, due to manipulation, people will
question the authenticity of images. I doubt
people will ever abandon their traditional belief in
the image. I think you'd know a manipulated
image when you saw one."

"For instance, take the first portrait photographs.
You had to stay still for 10 minutes; I'd call that
manipulation as well."

"It wasn't out of the norm in Soviet Russia to
erase a *persona non grata* from a picture."

"If people accept that images can be manipulated,
it doesn't imply they will question everything."

"These days everyone has a camera, a video
camera and a computer."

"I don't."

"Well, you're a little retarded, aren't you?"

"Okay, I'm a retard. I don't have a video camera, I don't even want one. I only take snapshots."

"Usually I prefer coffee after dinner."

"I'd like a cappuccino."

"Another example; ask a hundred people to go and see a movie, then ask them what they saw. Will you get a hundred different answers?"

"Oh, you mean a Gauss curve."

"What curve?"

"A Gauss curve. Don't you know the principle of the Gauss curve? Hang on, give me a pen. Here is the y-axis, here the x-axis, this is the Gauss curve. It looks like a classic bowler hat. Whatever you measure: strength, intelligence, movement, the results will always be a Gauss curve. There's a large group in the middle, and on either side a small group, the brim."

"Send a hundred people to the cinema. Most will have seen the same thing, but a few will say 'It was about Hitler', others will say 'No, it was all about Shirley Temple.' Regardless of the subject of your research, the result could always translate in a Gauss curve."

"Confused? You've never heard of this before?"

"The law of mediocrity."

"This isn't about quality."

"No, about Gauss's curve."

"A bowler hat, nothing underneath, nothing around."

WONDERLAND JUNGLE II

traffic jam, fog, may flowers, hot chocolate, a missed turn-off

"Do you always get so uptight about those lousy
articles in the papers?"
"That's a bit vague."
"You're testing my patience."
"How do you mean?"
"Commentaries, you know the type."
"Shall we agree to drop discussions about
quality today?"
"Huh?"
"Can't we, for once, moan about all those
second-rate journalists?"
"I got to be somewhere later."
"Alright, fair enough."
"In my opinion there's a difference between the
amount of time spent on something and the level
of appreciation."
"Isn't that a bit obvious."
"Not so long ago I spoke with a writer about the
difference between word and image."
"Tut-tut."
"He pointed out that the Net clearly shows what
is happening with images. Downloaded, one after
the other, copied, you can do whatever you like
with them. Easy peasy. Language doesn't give you
that freedom. It cannot be copied endlessly. You
need at least three pages to make your point."
"A picture says more than three pages."
"Words are thought to be a bigger threat
than images."
"So, images were never taken as seriously or
considered as interesting as language. You can do
whatever you want with them."
"Especially since you could always manipulate
them."
"Really?"
"From Hieronymus Bosch's demons to cheap
computer manipulations."

"Because of his book, Salman Rushdie was persecuted. Persecuted because of his words."

"Could images provoke persecution?"

"Yes and no, that is the paradox. A picture is a thousand words, isn't it? If you had to describe the Mona Lisa, a book wouldn't suffice, even a hefty one. All you'd need is an image."

"Any idea why that is?"

"Maybe it could be due to the fact that some religions have prohibited images since the dawn of time."

"Which religions?"

"Portrayal has sometimes been prohibited, be it of a human or a god. That has been the rule, people have always hesitated breaking it. On the other hand, books were often burnt. Painters and sculptors..."

"Iconoclasm?"

"Icons. Yes, but they burnt icons. Writers are persecuted. I cannot think of any painter that was ever persecuted. For some reason or another, dictators always feared the written word, rather than the image."

"Simultaneously, an image is thought to be more powerful, there's our paradox."

"What a dilemma for the artist."

"Yes, you couldn't be more right."

"Have you experienced that when going to museums?"

"No, that's the funny thing."

"I keep on walking till I come across an artwork that for one reason or another makes me stop."

"What happens next?"

"I take a look."

"How long does your look last?"

"5 to 10 minutes, maybe half an hour."

"I don't have that kind of endurance. Sometimes I time myself and on average I've never got past 30 seconds."

"There are some works of art you can look at for ages."

"Rembrandt's self-portrait at the Rijksmuseum in Amsterdam."

"Absolutely sublime."

"I could look at that till time stood still."

"Not me. I could look at it many times, that's the difference."

"That's why I like benches in museums."

"Every time I see a work like that, I see something different."

"Half an hour..."

"I often find artworks too severe. Art is a crude means of expression. It's devoid of time."

"Above all, literature is linked to time."

"That's what's so absurd. It takes a painter two years to make a painting, and I take a minute at the most to look at it. A writer needs two years to write a book, it takes me, say, six hours to read it."

"And then?"

"Then I think it's a wonderful book."

"But it is very unlikely that you will re-read it soon after."

"That's not the point."

"You could go see that same painting 20 times."

"Is that the shopkeeper in you?"

"20 times one minute adds up to no more than 20 minutes. Six hours spent reading a book, is 6 times 60 minutes, making a grand total of 360 minutes."

"It seems given that an artist deals with time in a way that he catches your attention for as long as possible."

"Can't we just gossip about that stupid article on the latest fads in art in last week's paper?"

"I'm afraid I have to be strict today."

"You're always being strict."

"A writer publishes a book. To discover whether I like the book, I spend, let's say, two hours with it."

"How much time do you spend looking at the artwork on your living room wall?"

"Visual art is more demanding than literature."

"I think it is more demanding. It's just like holidays. You only get 25 days a year. You book three weeks in Tunisia. Even if it were the worst holiday you ever had, you would still say it was great. So much money and especially so much time."

"For status?"

"When I finish a book, I wouldn't say I was bored stiff. That's not the case with the artwork. Relatively speaking I've hardly spent time and energy on it."

"It seems as if you confuse the amount of time spent on it with the quality of it."

"I'm only talking about the difference between time spent on something and the level of appreciation for it."

"More time doesn't equate to appreciation."

"That's too difficult."

"The effect of time."

"We're not discussing quality."

"Oh no, only the Gauss's curve principle."

"A bowler hat, nothing underneath, nothing around."

THE WHITE HOLE

I HAVE A PASSION FOR FACTORIES. They are often dull and drab on the outside, while inside the production process radiates a buzz of excitement on to the shopfloor. Though they may pretend to be nothing more than functional structures, built simply to produce a product, for me they are unacclaimed monuments. Straightforwardly, without fuss, they reflect the time they were built. I'm so fascinated by them that it doesn't mean a thing that most will never win a beauty contest.

The first factories in England appeared at the beginning of the nineteenth century and developed over the next hundred years. One great example is the Linotype factory. It sits in a typically English landscape on the top of a hill. The buildings resemble meticulously maintained feudal castles. There's no sign of heavy labour, trucks or industrial activity. Lawns stretch between the buildings and there is even a cricket pitch for the employees. Linotype is known for the presses that they produce, which are all assembled in fairly small rooms. Each worker is given responsibility for the entire production of a machine from start to finish. He develops a genuine involvement in the manufacturing process, and you could actually see the factory as a collection of workshops. The heavy pieces of cast iron and innumerable mechanical parts that are produced elsewhere, are neatly stored in nearby warehouses. The machines seem indestructible and the factory emits an air of tranquillity and thorough craftsmanship, apparently relying on old traditions that could not be improved.

Conversely, the factories built at the beginning of this century evoke an image of mass production, hard work, neglect and squalor. The appearance of the buildings is irrelevant to the process, they all tend to be quite tall, with sawtooth roofs. Today, they seem neglected, scabby and unpainted.

A penetrating yet romantic scent welcomes you—even before you've caught sight of the chamois leather factory. The façade is a mess—the name of the factory in thick black letters, an ill-defined hall, a porter's lodge in front of a dilapidated brick building. Barrels and crates full of brined sheepskins sit in the front yard—the raw material for the production of the chamois leather cloths.
Inside, rusty machines rest on their last legs. Water is everywhere—it's filthy. Here the sheepskins are washed and soaked in chemical baths. Once saturated, they swell and are then split in two. The combination of

chemicals and water slowly corrodes the machines. In the rear of the hall, the skins are treated with train oil in gigantic vats, the smell permeating the entire building. The workers are clad in dark blue overalls with shiny rubber aprons and wellington boots.

The combination of the product, the noise, the people, and the neglected buildings feels like a factory from the 20s, though the reality is that many of the machines are now computer-controlled—so much for romance.

In the dry spaces, the final product is chafed and sorted by size and quality. These are places sinking under the weight of piles of chamois leather, with all the workmen covered in dust. Yet the chamois leathers are so beautiful you immediately forget the decay and the dirt. Their wonderful yellow colour and unbelievable softness seduce you into believing the acrid stench has become a sensuous scent. Their sheer quantity keeps alive those romantic dreams crushed by the computerised control. A single object, repeated *ad infinitum*, always appeals.

To visit a brick factory is a completely different experience. They are always situated near a river and resemble nothing so much as an automated farm. From a distance, the low buildings look like barn houses and animal sheds. In the centre of the complex is an open court filled with bricks on pallets waiting to be shipped out. Alone in the landscape, an old dragline digs up the clay. A small trolley brings it to a large mixer where it is then squeezed into moulds and set to dry in one of the buildings. The buildings are full of holes to let the wind whip through and turn the clay into bricks. Inside, the pinpoints of daylight create a secretive, dusky atmosphere. After a few weeks, the clay is removed from the moulds and the bricks are put into one of six narrow, deep ovens.

The entire site is very rural, there are few labourers and it's a simple process. It is not hard to imagine that these factories will still be exactly the same in a hundred years' time.

The soap factory is a nondescript building. You can't tell from the exterior what is produced there. Even inside it is not very clear how the process works as there seems to be no logical order. The building is divided into two sections. One, a laboratory where the scents, colours and shapes of the soap bars are determined. Here are the usual array of test-tubes, bottles, bowls and shelves for chemicals, essences and pigments tended to by a few employees in white coats. The other section—three huge interconnected halls—is the actual factory. A maze of pipes runs everywhere. The main ingredient is an already prepared and solidified oil that resembles flakes of lard. Vast quantities of this oil are mixed in huge tubs, transported through pipes into other tubs and then forced through a series of different treatments. Eventually the viscous mass ends up as a thick paste on a conveyor belt, from where it is squeezed into moulds and made ready for packing. The soap residue around the moulds is returned to the beginning for another run through the process. Several labourers control the machines and whatever happens along the conveyor belt. It is all very boring, the only seduction being the final product in use. It seems as though the factory is nothing more than a tool, left outside for too long—rusty but still working.

The most surprising thing is that the factory buildings actually change their appearance. By the 60s, the sawtooth roof with its regulation height and style has disappeared. Factories become more sophisticated, with fountains in front and, eventually, a 'turd in the plaza'. A similar story can be told about the development of machinery. Before a certain moment, the working parts of cars, trams and industrial equipment were visible. Then, in the name of safety and aerodynamic efficiency, everything was hidden behind protective shields and colourful skins. Even the workers become completely unrecognisable in their anti-dust clothing. It's also becoming more difficult to visit a factory, supposedly out of fear of the competition, all the formulae, processes and tricks of the trade are now stored behind locked doors.

Contemporary factories have been unable to resist the threat of standardisation. They all look the same. Europe is overrun with anonymous, grey boxes standing along the highway. Each company has its standard design, red or blue window sills and plenty of dark glass in the office area. Supposedly standardisation serves our convenience but I find it hard to believe it was meant to lead to this overwhelming uniformity. Especially when you consider that this same standard has limited our choices to such a huge extent. For instance, if I want an odd-sized steel bar with a particular diameter, it can only be ordered in vast quantities and at great expense. I am punished for wanting something different.

The time of the palaces of production is long past. A different era has emerged, led by ergonomics, efficiency and sustainability. Products, particularly from heavy industry, are needed less and less. Shipyards, steel factories and coal mines have all virtually disappeared from Europe. Factories have now become the subject of nostalgic photographs—a sure sign of history having run its course.

In Duisburg, however, an attempt has been made to close that circle. In the heart of the industrial Ruhr area, a factory has become a contemporary cultural site in its own right. A bankrupt steel factory has been transformed into a park—without the removal of any of the original buildings. The imposing towers, heavy machinery, cooling vats, rail tracks and hangars have been interspersed with new trees. Rather than using the standard wooden poles, the saplings are supported by rusty iron beams. The whole area has been declared a sculpture park and the designers have remained very conscious of the quality and beauty of the industrial buildings. They created a park in which the steel and iron ruins are respected for their own sake and the site is left for us to explore.

Eighty-one cast iron slabs form an immense 'lawn', surrounded by an apparently traditional border. It's hard to believe human hands ever built this. As a visitor you can go places where once only workers were allowed to enter.

Great heaps of electrical wiring can still be found in the hangars. The scale of one pipe here is like 100 pipes anywhere else, its size is simply incomprehensible. The same can be said for the buildings. They are extraordinarily complex because of the enormous amount of machinery they contain. You can't even discern their contours, they appear to be gigantic pieces of coral. You need more than one pair of eyes.

In the centre of the park is a tower, 60 metres high, from which you can see the entire layout. The tower is also full of machinery and is a museum in itself. The only thing you miss is the sound of clanking machines —a silence made all the more obvious by the birds singing outside.

The trees are not yet fully grown, though I can imagine what this park will look like in 20 years time. Trees will start to compete with the enormous iron structures, which will eventually become sculptures supporting and decorating nature. Perhaps this 'garden' might turn into an impromptu Generalife.

The original casting floor is now the stage of a simple open-air theatre. The only thing added is a concrete terrace and some theatre lights, as if you were sitting in another Colosseum. This park is on a par with any ancient Greek or Roman site and could also be easily mistaken for a work by Piranesi. The difference being that history has been fast-forwarded.

Only three years ago, the machines were brought to a halt, and already the park has become an unacknowledged monument. There seems to be no time between one state and another any more. The end of an era merges with its revaluation.

1.16
THE CYLINDER CORRECTOR

The obligation to confess is felt from so many sources, that it really has become second nature, and we don't experience it as being put under pressure anymore.

1.23
CARL UYTTERHAGEN

He sarcastically talks about the "obscene pleasure with which significance reigns in the harem of things, as if it were a perverse sultan".

TRAILS   off
RAIN   off
SUPPRESS   off
BLANKING   off
AREA   2
ZOOM   off

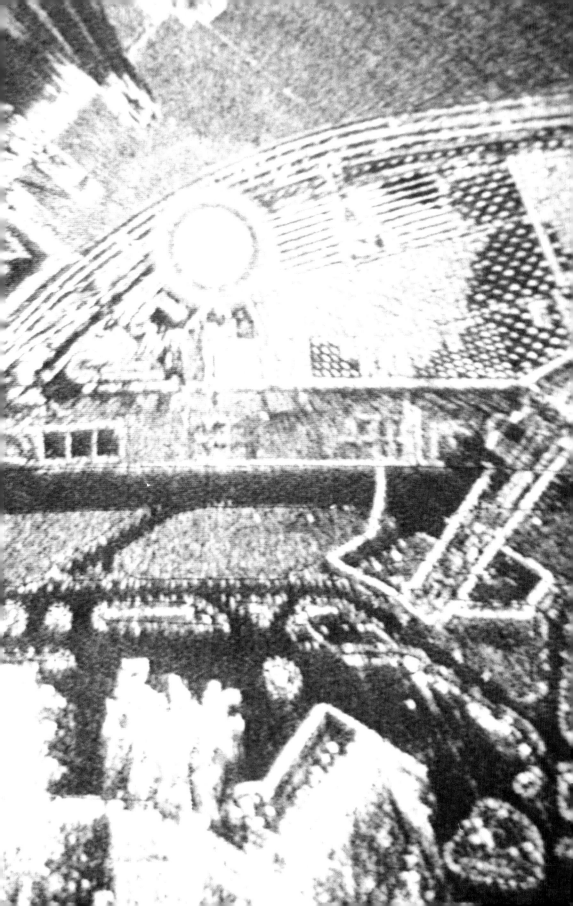

THE JET BLAST COOLING PUMP II

- (Tuesday 06.24) -

I'm riding in a pick-up truck along a winding road. A pile of junk fills the back—blankets, crates, boxes, I've no idea what's in them. Alongside me in the cab there are two or three friends—the director of a shady 'Save the Whales' foundation, an insurance broker and, I think, a female estate agent. There's an air of recklessness.

We're on our way from A to B, not even knowing where A was or B will be. Despite our increasing speed, the coat and a fat wallet on the bonnet don't move.

Before I get used to this scene, we reach a beautiful green forest cut by a single-track railway. We walk along the tracks, enjoying the silence and tranquillity. It's impossible to get lost in such an environment. Then suddenly the forest becomes a beach. I'm just about to tell my fellow travellers how calm the sea looks, when we're caught by a tidal wave. We survive and kill ourselves laughing. Then we play a game following the edge of the high tide along the remaining strip of beach, avoiding the enormous waves that sweep towards us. A different company, a windless storm, an absence of cold.

- (Wednesday 11.09) -

A hand wrapped in a rubber glove. A piece of ear with tufts of black hair. Strange parts of machinery, red against a background of steam and fire. At least two-hundred motors, all the same colour, installed next to each other in an industrial park. A view from above on the Vehicle Assembly Building complete with infrastructure and security towers.

A view on an unremarkable city. I don't have the faintest idea which city or country. To the left a woman in a grey dress cycles past, her entire face covered with an orange veil. Why does she protect herself? A series of picturesque images passes my eyes at high speed. Jumping dolphins, bubbling waterfalls, wooded landscapes, romantic sunsets, a mountain covered with everlasting snow and a babbling brook in the foreground. Views of fields carpeted in flowers, hundreds of goldfish skimming the surface of a beautiful pond. The images become more anonymous; details of the structure of a leaf, a flag-pole seen from the base, the hide of an animal, a piece of cloth. Rubbish, empty floors, a completely stripped house, a deserted hospital ward.

It's almost impossible to grasp the series of miniscule enlargements that follows. I can't describe the images, I don't know what they are. Less light, less colour. Reversed images, some of them so complex it's impossible to dissect them. Indeterminable colours and shapes, mixed without logic or meaning. A different kind of interpretation emerges. White light, a surface into which I would immediately like to throw myself.

- (Thursday 03.53) -

Watching the oncoming traffic, you will soon start searching for exceptions —an old car, a strange text, an odd colour. Our eternal quest for the exceptional is nothing less than an effort to try and grasp the structure of what we see. The same thing happens when you're walking in the country. You look for human traces, fences, railings, telephone-poles, houses. You aren't interested in the exceptions as such, only in the confirmation of their existence.

Last night I went to a park by the river. What caught my eye at first were all the people walking their dogs. It looked like a public gathering with the dogs as go-betweens. The field was full of them, right there in the heart of New York.

Half a day later it happens again. I'm driving around and by accident I end up near the Olympic stadium. For once, it is possible to gain access and I find myself completely alone in a 72,000-seater amphitheatre. A little foggy, the last remains of snow. I am enthralled by the vastness, especially as it doesn't seem to matter whether anything has happened or will ever happen here. This moment of expectation is what fascinates me. Maybe nothing ever happened, maybe things are about to happen, but now it is empty. For a brief moment all of the 72,000 seats belong to me, not in actuality, but through the experience of an in-between moment. In the end the skeleton is more interesting than the flesh. Maybe that's what it's all about. The potential of things or the moments before they take shape.

- (Friday) -

Nothing received.

- (Saturday 08.44) -

The N7—smoothly, closer than I thought. There are clues: Amsterdam/ Hengelo/Osnabrück/Hannover/Berlin. Every time you pass a sign it gives you the distance to the next city—200, 150, 37. They're so tempting, after all 200 kilometres is not that far. All those signs form a grid that covers the entire continent. Scale and distance are related to the human scale, a measure than can be bridged, controlled. You notice the transition from West to East because of the recent widening of the narrow roads and the number of new flyovers. Other than that you can hardly tell the difference. Arrival is exciting. What is the structure of this city? Is there any difference between the former East and West Berlin?

Berlin is wide. There's so much space everywhere, so many broad green streets. The architecture of the western suburb of Charlottenburg is reminiscent of that of any nineteenth-century city. East Berlin is simpler, old, badly maintained but definitely more interesting and full of potential—still an in-between area that breathes more freely. In several years this will all be forgotten, the past will be swallowed by the eternal thirst for progress. Neat signs will then point the way to the monuments of the past.

- *(Sunday 13.39)* -

I find myself on a terrace close to the water, surrounded by beautiful industrial buildings. People are diving off the quay and the sound of their laughter can be heard far away. Nearby a bridge leads to the oldest part of the city, high on a small island. Everywhere tourists are taking the typical pictures. The weather is beautiful, though in the distance clouds foreshadow a shower. A man is trying to impress two girls by performing tricks in his small rubber dinghy. Guests on the terrace are slightly perturbed. Soon after the man drags his boat up onto the bridge and dives off. I hardly dare look. A splash, then laughter. One of the girls has fallen out of the boat and tries to climb aboard again.

Suddenly there is a rumbling noise to my left. The sounds get louder and louder. It's as though an ocean liner is heading for the citadel at full speed. But there is no ship, just a big cloud of dust. Suddenly the whole island starts moving. One square mile of rock slips quietly and elegantly into the water like a capsized ship. Breathtaking. Nearer to me entire buildings spin round on their axis and disappear, gracefully, almost without a sound.

Probably because of the slow beauty of the scene, I forget to check if I am still standing on safe ground. People around me don't make any noise, they don't scream. Simultaneously a huge building behind me disappears into the water. It's as though the laws of gravity have dissolved. Thinking as quickly as I can, I take a deep breath and hope that I can swim up to the surface. Suddenly it is as dark as night. Apparently I am caught up in a huge air bubble. From this moment on my thoughts are vague. The dream stops before I know whether I have escaped.

I.3

JACQUES VAN COUWENBERGHE

There is always a difference between the subject as expressed in a sentence and the subject who produces the sentence, the format being a temporary position adopted within the process of the latter.

1.37

PAUL VAN DEN NOORDGATE

He has summarised the basic pattern of his historical approach in a methodical reflection, that, as a 'construction', presupposes a 'deconstruction'.

ÎLE FLOTTANTE OR
FLOATING ISLAND

"Could you imagine uniting your study into the nature of the world with the concept of the jester or fool?"
"It would certainly turn a lot of things upside down."
"Would Stephen Hawking fit in here?"
"No."
"Why not?"
"Because I don't understand his faith in the scientific process."
"Faith.... Literally?"
"I think it's literal for him. He says he's looking for God's masterplan."
"I disagree with that."
"It's such a romantic idea—trying to solve the problems of the world—when there is no solution."
"The principles behind his ideas and his terminology will never lead to a solution. It's like looking up the meaning of an English word in a Dutch-German dictionary. You'll get close, but no cigar."
"Yes."
"So, there are limitations?"
"When you say limitations, do you really mean limitations? Why not use it as a starting point?"
"Eventually Hawking got stuck."
"I'm really into pre-Christian religions at the moment."
"Didn't he want to make megaliths?"
"Mega-whats?"
"You know, structures marking the ground, like Stonehenge, or the temples in Mexico."
"No, I don't."
"That sounds more like a Robert Smithson to me."
"Not really. Smithson dealt with entropy."

"And entropy has got nothing to do with sacred grounds, or the creation of sacred monuments."
"He made a film about his work *Spiral Jetty*, from a helicopter. Up in the air, he wanted to be in the centre of the sun, while filming the work."
"Didn't that cause the crash that killed him?"
"The perfect death for an artist!"
"In the midst of a struggle with his own work. Beautiful."
"The James Dean principle."
"You also see the failure. In terms of entropy I can imagine he was interested in the spiral."
"I adore his *Study for a floating island around Manhattan*."
"Hmmm."
"Could you explain the word entropy for me?"
"For scientists it is the second law of thermodynamics."
"For me it's the principle that all the energy needed to be born equates the energy neccessary to live and die."
"So actually there's no development, no progress."
"But we still grow up with the idea that paradise exists. And that there is a linear development in our culture."
"I don't really like having sex every day."
"Really?"
"Everything always seem to get better, but in the end it's all the same. It changes a little, then again it doesn't change at all."
"Things move."
"Just the form, slightly."
"Another cigarette?"
"Back to entropy. Without development, we'd still be wearing bear skins, though plenty of shops on Madison Avenue seem to have missed that point."
"So the whole idea of entropy doesn't apply."
"If I were to show you my idea of entropy, I'd use a series of circles, merging here and there."
"Minor changes?"
"Movement."

"One circle to the other."

"Of course, the spaces in between are far more interesting than the circles themselves. The points where two circles meet are intriguing. There you can see two different worlds, two different spaces, you're just an observer."

"Sounds pretty close to your idea of entropy."

"The best combination of circles is, of course, the so-called parallactic triangle."

"Isn't a parallactic triangle a triangle with three concave... or is it convex, sides?"

"This triangle basically illustrates my way of thinking. I usually talk about black holes, which again is an idea snatched from science."

"Time for another beer."

"The concept of the black holes epitomises the idea of entropy. Illustrating the scientific concept that all energy vanishes."

"Not even light can escape."

"Are you serious?"

"Call me romantic, but the words that spring to mind are Paradise and Escape."

"Hmmm... interesting. I think of a Hoover."

"I once saw Stephen Hawking give a lecture. The topic was black holes. At the end he explained about the huge forces of gravity around them. A gravity so strong that time itself is stretched. His theory was that if a particle was sucked into the black hole that, due to entropy, it would eventually have to come out somewhere, sometime."

"I've never put much stock into the idea of the all-encompassing black hole. That's what I call the Hoover principle."

"The sack gets full."

"I guess the black hole is actually a tunnel. A tunnel to a different dimension. I once came across a book with a reproduction of the Einstein-Rosen Bridge. I didn't really know what it meant, but it was the perfect illustration of the black hole principle."

"Perhaps for us it's unfathomable that one day we will be able to go through that tunnel. But maybe

it's the next stop on the intergallactic highway."
"Entropy, black holes, Einstein-Rosen Bridges,
they're all back to the starting point of being
in-between. What I'm interested in is being at the
borderline—between two different ideas or two
different cultures."
"How about illustrating that with a dinner."
"Excuse me?"
"Simple. You're hungry, so you peck on olives,
crackers, bread. You order some wine. If the
waiter is smart enough, you're drunk before you
know it. Then the first course arrives. You dig
straight in, until your initial craving is satiated.
The real meal has yet to come. You're in the
midst of a conversation with your dining
companions. All waiting, you know that there's
more to come. You can relax, smoke a cigarette,
order more wine. At this point the conversation
starts to become interesting. It's a moment that I
really love—this bizarre 'in-between' situation,
you're no longer concerned with what brought
you there to begin with—to eat. You know more
food is on its way, which gives you the chance to
move again, with no apparent aim. Once you try
to focus, movement ceases. If you look for the
borders, you'll never find them. But actually I'm
hungry now. How about you?"
"No, not really."
"I am."
"Are you always hungry?"
"Hawking's conclusion—which is relevant to what
you've said—is that black holes could be means of
time travel. Not from one dimension to the other,
but from one time to another."
"The interesting thing is that he's so focused on
time, which is his speciality. Because it is
scientifically impossible to visualise the universe."
"Forget about science, I just use my imagination
and make up stories."
"Which is a fun thing to do."
"They don't mean that much, but there's always

someone willing to listen."

"Of course, Smithson would have done the same."

"I wouldn't go that far."

"By the way, I like your green T-shirt."

"Why?"

"It's a beautiful colour."

TRAILS   off
RAIN   off
SUPPRESS   off
TRACKING   off
ZOOM   x2

LES FONCTIONNAIRES ET LES PERCEPTEURS

Let's play war.
   I'm the general and you're the martyr.
Sirens wail.
Take shelter, tremble, stay put.
War has begun.
Without any warning.
Fall back: shore up the attic.
The first wave of resistance rounded up.
Mercilessly.
Everyone a winner.
The time of terror is over.
We have survived.
Catch the traitors, string them up, teach them a lesson.
Especially my quisling neighbour.

WHERE ONE DREAMS OF THE FRAIL GIRL ON HER BIKE, THE
TALL BLONDE ONE WITH THE DARK GREEN EYES, THE NAVEL
OF THERESA, THE COUSIN FROM AMERICA, THE HORNY GLANCE
OF THE WOMAN BEHIND THE COUNTER, THE CURRENT
GIRLFRIEND'S YOUNGER SISTER, ERECTIONS AND ORGASMS,
THE BEAUTIFULL BREASTS OF JEANINE, HELENA'S ARMS,
ELLEN'S HAIR, IRENE'S MOUTH AND CECILE'S PUBIC HAIR.

- *The moment* -

The day is over.
Low sunset.
A man dives into the water from a diving board.
A short movement, a sound, a slight change of scent, an interruption in the
smoothness of the water's surface.
The moment almost too brief to experience.
The same man, this time on the high diving board.
Standing quietly, concentrating. He sprints to the edge and jumps.
A salto mortale followed by a double screw.
A fraction of a second.
Splashing water, sound, a slight change of scent, the surface breaks.
Almost too brief to experience.
Too brief to see it properly, too brief to remember, too brief to judge the
difference.

WHERE ONE IS WARNED ABOUT PICKPOCKETS AND ROBBERS, TEDDY BOYS, PAEDOPHILES, CHILDREN AND UNLEASHED DOGS, ROLLERSKATERS ROLLING PAST, MONSTERS, SALESMEN, CHANTING SUPPORTERS, TRAMPS, POLITICIANS, FORGERS, DRUNKEN STUDENTS, MASQUERADES AND PARTIES, NEIGHBOURS AND FAMILY MEMBERS, SMART ALECS AND SWINDLERS, CIVIL SERVANTS AND TAX COLLECTORS.

- The experience -

She was standing next to me, not knowing what she was watching.
Was it an illusion or did she have something in her eye? As if different images interfered and merged with each other.
Was she a victim of tricks, holograms or computer manipulation?
Wincing, trying to focus but seeing only a continuously moving stage set with too many actors. Irritated that she couldn't see what she was looking at—no recognition, no clues.
Everything seemed to evaporate. Amazed at how sight influenced the way she thought, how different she now felt.
Time, distance and scale were no longer distinguishable.
Colours changed their meaning, matter seemed to vanish.
Initially she was scared and tried to resist. Later she started to enjoy it.
Her thoughts happier, her pace more relaxed, her surroundings whirling.
She was beautiful and became even more so, there, next to me.

WHERE ONE IS URGENTLY REQUESTED TO BEAR IN MIND THAT OPENING HOURS HAVE CHANGED, NOT TO USE RUDE LANGUAGE, TO WEAR A TIE, NOT TO DRINK ANY ALCOHOL, TO EMPATHISE WITH OTHERS, TO BEHAVE DECENTLY, NOT TO KISS HIS OR HER LOVER IN PUBLIC, TO FOLLOW DIRECTIONS, TO LOOK NO-ONE STRAIGHT IN THE EYE, TO STRICTLY FOLLOW THE HOUSE RULES.

- The impossibility of experience -

I dreamt about an escape route last night. I found myself in a huge house where I had never been before. By a small entrance, a massive wooden relief hung on the wall.
Thoughtlessly I walked up to one of the protruding panels and pulled it down. I pressed the strange-looking button that emerged.
Looking into a black hole that appeared to be an entrance.
I can't remember whether I actually went in.
Suddenly I find myself by the side of an Italian square, looking at the same house, now from the outside.

Shaped like a long box with an extremely big, pointed roof, the last building left on the fringe of an immense square.
Its long wall slowly transformed into perfectly transparent glass, dissolving in its surroundings so completely you could hardly speak of its disappearance.
Only the square remained.
Empty, water in the distance.

WHERE ONE THINKS ABOUT SKYSCRAPERS AND OFFICE BUILDINGS, FACTORIES AND BUSINESS CENTRES, INDUSTRIAL AND RESIDENTIAL AREAS, PARKS AND GARDENS, SCHOOLS AND LEISURE CENTRES, EMBASSIES AND CONCERT BUILDINGS, CITY HALLS AND ZOOS, CHURCHES AND HOSPITALS, STATIONS AND SQUARES, HIGH-RISE BUILDINGS AND FAMILY HOUSES, SHOPS AND WORKSHOPS, APARTMENTS AND PIEDS-À-TERRE.

- *The place* -

Tens of birdcages with twittering canaries decorate the entrance. Amongst them one lonely parrot.
A large, round room with pillars and a concave floor. Behind each pillar, a smaller, cylindrical room. At three different points the rooms converge inexplicably into the large room.
Complete circles don't exist.
Searching for a centre, for a point where you could grasp the room, or rather the rooms, automatically starting to walk, carefully. Convoluted pillars, their details so elaborate that they become almost morbid, the scale overwhelming, prompting a slight distrust.
Withdrawal is not an option. The experience wouldn't have been any less enjoyable with a slighty less abundant display.
An eternal battle between ultimate pleasure and reason.
Pleasure wins, fortunately.
Especially when you discover slowly that the richness has nothing to do with decoration or decorum, but apparently serves a purpose, though one that cannot be described.
The sun is a parallactic triangle, the glow an autonomous movement, independent from its source.
Hang on to your vertigo.

WHERE ONE OBSERVES THE PYRAMIDS AND THE EIFFEL TOWER, THE TOWER OF PISA OR DEVOTIONAL PICTURES, GLASSES WITH INSCRIPTIONS, THE CHALICE WITH THE TOWN ARMS, PRINTED SCARVES AND WICKER BASKETS, SILVER TEASPOONS AND ASHTRAYS, THE FRAMED PORTRAIT OF THE LOCAL KING, LEATHER PURSES, PLAYING CARDS WITH NUDES, BANGLES, BAGS, STONE BOXES AND INFINITE NUMBERS OF POSTCARDS.

- The impossibility of place -

Everyone appeared excited. Cheering anxiously, awaiting our guide who had promised us that this would be the *moment suprême* of this excursion. Then he gave us the usual information, dates, wars and natural disasters. If you were unaware of the original function of this place, you would never have guessed.

We looked at old, weather-beaten architecture, commanding respect because of its age. It was difficult for us to describe the particularity of this place, more so since we were to visit other, similar places. However, our guide didn't label those as *moments suprêmes*, nor were they mentioned in our travelogue.

Sooner or later you just can't help but feel indifferent.

WHERE IT IS PROHIBITED TO TALK LOUDLY, TO SPIT, TO STEP ON THE GRASS, TO BURGLE, TO THREATEN TO KILL ONE'S NEIGHBOUR, TO SMOKE, TO DANCE, TO CURSE, TO PARK, TO STEAL, TO DESTROY, TO PLAY WAR, TO DROWN ONE'S MOTHER, TO BOTHER LITTLE GIRLS, TO LET YOUR THOUGHTS WANDER, TO STICK OUT YOUR NECK.

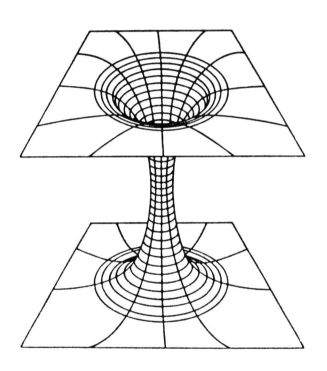

THE MAECENAS SAW THE LIGHT
FLICKERING—A PLEA

IN THE POKER GAME OF CULTURE, all the aces seem to have been dealt to the visual. The media have won the fight for cultural hegemony, but only by making up the rules to suit themselves. Time and distance, necessary for original ideas to develop, are eradicated. 'Innovation' has more to do with speed and connecting fragments appropriated from a host of various 'originators'. Hence 'innovation' seems to have become the territory of curators, media producers, and other 'predators'. However, as long as humans stick to their primeval need for form *and* content, it will eventually become clear that this 'innovation' occurs on only one level—the appearance of form.

A good example is the revaluation of the 50s, or rather, the speed with which revaluations succeed one another. Mondrian-esque embellishments on shampoo bottles or cheap frocks provide a sense of recognition. It makes us feel a little more in control of our over-confusing present. This visual recycling makes it easier for designers to create new trends year in year out. The same can be said of the other 'predators', falling back on the past when devoid of new ideas. Even the young benefit, they don't have to bother to explore what happened 10, 20 or 30 years ago. In 1983 the recycling of the past extended over a period of about twenty years, now I wait with anticipation for the year 1995—when the revaluation of 1995 simultaneously takes place.

This must be one of the most exciting periods in history. Could it be that the artist lost absolute power over his work, and now answers directly to the commands of culture? He is likely to be judged on terms that apply in other fields. The ever-increasing speed with which 'new' trends come and go is simple proof. The creator is dismissed as quickly as he arrived. Thank God I love B-movies. Their perpetually recurring love stories serve as a genuine antidote to the accelerating innovation machine.

The audience has also changed. All we have now is one stratum—the omnipresent middle class. But even this audience can no longer be taken for granted. Sometimes they grow so bold as to denounce the shenanigans of the art circus. The artists who disguise their lack of talent are easier to expose. However exciting they appear, even the use of labyrinths is an attempt at disguise, it is only by allowing yourself to get lost that you get a chance to detect the quality in a work of art. Whether or not the image is visualised is no longer of importance.

That said, to avoid disappointing the audience with the artist's failure, his guilt or, even worse still, his penance, it is intrinsic that a work of art be visually appealing. But the appeal opposes direct contact with the image, leading the viewer astray.

Like the shock of a kiss without seeing a face.
Meaning seems to dissolve.

The mirror no longer reflects, but receives.

3.14
STROMBOLI

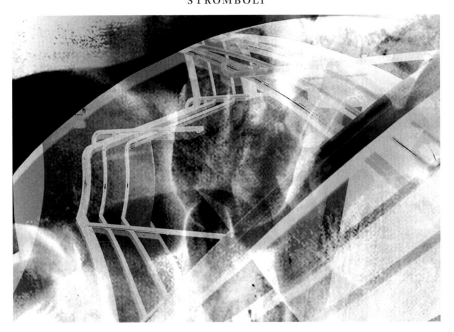

The North Pole is always on that side of the solenoide from which the lines of force emerge. Hence, the magnetic power of a solenoide is exactly the same as that of an ordinary magnet.

3.38
AÎX-LES-BAINS

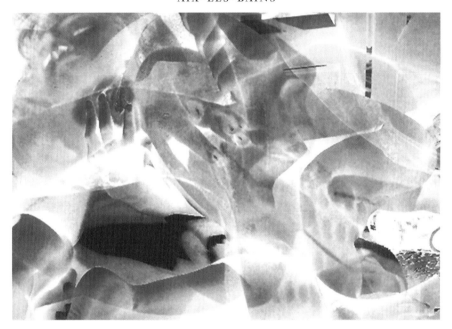

The atom can only exist in the appearances that mechanics allow; whilst in one of those states, it doesn't emit radiation.

THE MIRACLE

Left-hand dialogue

"I believe in miracles, and much, much more."

"The way you ask that question sounds like you believe in utopia."

"Well, I have to say that the change we hoped for was no change at all. But still everything is in motion. I'm happy about that. The desire for change brought about too much pressure."

"These days utopians have all turned into confirmed pessimists. That doesn't mean that their yearning for utopia has diminished. On the contrary, that is exactly what prevents the possibility of change."

"Are you suggesting that if you let go of the desire for change, you initiate a situation where change is possible?"

"Behind closed doors."

"Art behind closed doors?"

"It's only natural that art should be out in the open whenever possible, but that has nothing to do with change. The given link between art and flux doesn't really exist. Art doesn't necessarily equal change."

"Shouldn't art be unsettling, disconcerting... shocking, even?"

"Exactly, and there's not much art that..."

"Oh yeah, it's all quite beautiful, isn't it."

"Beauty is pure pleasure, depending on who uses the term."

"Right now superficiality is rampant. Not just in art, but everywhere."

"That doesn't mean that nothing is happening, it means that those who are really saying something are prone to being ignored."

"So, are you one of them?"

"That's a weird question. Tomorrow it will be different again. Just as long as things keep moving."

"A dilemma of artifice versus content?"

"That choice is up to the individual, and other factors such as money, power and prestige."

"A world of money, power and prestige is to be preferred?"

"The world in motion only knows 'l'Air du Temps'."

THE MIRACLE

Right-hand dialogue

"Do you believe in a better world?"

"I have to admit that my faith in utopia has been sorely tested."

"It's become tarnished. Twenty years ago I thought that anything was possible."

"You'd better be careful, people will be calling you a world-weary pessimist. Would you agree?"

"No, not at all. I think the longing for utopia has made way for a sense of reality that gives us the opportunity to let things happen."

"Behind closed doors, or screaming from the rooftops?"

"Years after hearing it for the first time, a good piece of music can take you back to where you first heard it. But no matter how close it comes to the source, it isn't real, it's only a memory, a record of our movements."

"Would you say that memory is part of what you call movement? Can you actually define movement?"

"For instance, take yourself. In the course of one day, you do many different things, your mood changes, and you react in different ways. The urge to arrange and order makes it impossible for you to accept the shifts."

"Would acceptance bring about the opposite of pessimism?"

"Sure, there are many beautiful things out there."

"Back to beauty?"

"Does that mean that you're giving in to that same one-dimensionality of perception and action?"

"No, of course that shallowness is there; but the form it takes becomes tarnished as soon as it emerges."

"Openings that allow interesting movements to happen, come up in these moments of appearing and disappearing."

"They flare up."

"And that's why you believe in miracles."

"And much, much more."

VILLA GIUSTO IN VERONA
TINTINHULL HOUSE IN SOMERSET

VILLA LANTE IN BAGNAIA
LE CLOS NORMAND IN GIVERNY
VILLA FARNESE IN CAPRAROLA
SISSINGHURST CASTLE GARDEN IN KENT
PECKOVER HOUSE, NEAR WISBECH
CHÂTEAU DE VILLANDRY IN TOURS
VILLA PALMIERI IN FIESOLE

HIDCOTE MANOR IN GLOUCESTERSHIRE
CASTELLO BALDUINO IN MONTALTO DI PAVIA

WHO'S NEXT?

Someone playing the bagpipes.

IMAGINE. WE ARE IN A ROUND BUILDING. Located in a beautiful spot with no name. Built with precision. It is said that it is a pleasure to be here. A building: six views, six windows, six statements. Imagine.

The second window

It's been many years since it was last painted. Not a hint of daylight, opened occasionally—to bring something in or to take something out. Meticulously lined up next to each other, in pairs, waiting for a possible journey. Some freshly polished, some with a dull shine. The rest carefully stretched with springs and wooden moulds. One pair, still in its fancy box, looks like the leader of the pack. Presumably the pair off to the side is the odd one out. Above this mass—clothes. Hanging precariously from a wooden stick, bending beneath their weight. Bulbous shapes, lying on a shelf, in the corner. Belts and ties hanging from a rope, stretched across the door. The shoes win. They are the proud carriers. You can read everything from them.

The third window

Step by step you rise. A soft carpet gives you the sensation that you're wearing trainers. Fingers curled around dark, carved wood. Smooth and shining with the scent of wax. Up, in the left-hand corner, a distorted window signals the imagination of the architect.

A small beam of light is all that is allowed to shine through. A mirror creates the illusion of space, portraying a completely different staircase, stretching further away. I see music, a waltz. Descent is unimaginable.

The existence of an artwork is a delicate matter. Old-fashioned, static, within spotless white boxes. You'd be fooling yourself if you thought they could compete with film, mass-produced products, bingo halls or dazzlingly lit amusement parks. Electronic technology offers such amazing views that the static artwork is quickly lost in the crowd. Ask yourself—does the image need to be animated, or make use of electronic technology? Perhaps we should move the museum itself into the laboratories of NASA. It's as pointless to deny this development in our culture, as it would be to abolish 'static' art. Facing this phenomenon, the artist's duty is to take a stand and attempt to offer an alternative.

The fourth window

Four comfortable chairs, gathered behind a pillar, covered in smiling cupids. To the left is a guest of some importance, judging by his shoes, face hidden behind a newspaper. Further to the left you catch a glimpse of a kitchen. Furnished with stainless steel appliances. The dark ceiling covered in atmospheric lights. Over to the right, a few suitcases, waiting, in front of a bar. In the foreground a small table with fancy cakes. It's difficult to resist the temptation.

The fifth window

Carefully arranged seats, row after row. Partly occupied by families and lone travellers. Luggage is scattered about—suitcases, trunks, carts, bags, you name it. A plain floor, and cylinders everywhere. On closer inspection they turn out to be glorified ashtrays. An empty counter. Above it a pricey monitor, showing times and destinations. There's glass and aluminium everywhere, shining. A cleaning machine with buckets full of foam. Blue suits, reading the *Wall Street Journal*, everywhere. Next to each chair the yellow bag, with the well-known logo, full of recent purchases. People double their pace on a conveyor belt. The frantic activity visible through the glass. For those waiting, a good enough reason to stay put.

With all this overload of information, the time to celebrate the transition of seasons is at hand. The treat is in the transition. A panoramic view —rear-view mirrors, completely nuts. Colour shifts, everything is in-between, red no longer red, blue no longer blue, yellow no longer yellow. Start the music, everybody dance. This is not a party for the faint-hearted, those with 'Yes... but', 'however' and 'nevertheless' need not reply. This is no celebration of the throwaway quote. No, it's going to be a party to celebrate change, a kaleidoscope of colours. The party has taken over, frivolous merriment abounds. Who cares about how it could be, should be, or would be. Here, let the good times roll.

A carnival of shifting opinions, cross-dressing and masquerades included. Long live beauty, beauty back, better than ever.

The sixth window

There's a hitch, when we discuss the unnameable. People hate it when things come without a label. If it's without a name they bend over backwards to give it one. Having said that, nothing is truely without a name. Picture this—I created a brand new shape. You would not be able to see it. You could only see it after having applied the Cow's Principle. Simply put, the

Cow's Principle is based on repetition, slowly bringing about a transformation. It's not the cow that changes, it's the grass it eats, digests and redigests until, eventually, milk is produced. The same principle applies to visual art. The strength of a brand new gesture enhances with repetition. The odd thing is that repetition is key to giving the unnameable its power, at the same time acquiring a name. Having said that, unnameability is just another word, and as such a name. It's nothing more than a flashlight illuminating something in the dark. It is definitely not the glowing Stone of Wisdom, if there ever were a glowing Stone of Wisdom. It's not about names, interpretations, or identifications. It's about change, about balancing. A juggler on a tightrope, preferably without a balancing pole.

The first window

Outside, a storm rages. Streetlights in the air, equidistant, lit but obscure. A mysterious glow announces the transition from day to night. Dusky skies, the sea a picture of chaos. Cresting waves form the lower part of the image, competing with the tablecloth and cruets. There's even a bolt of lightning. The dark sign 'Sea View' looks like a ship in distress. Glass screens apparently waving. White houses, against a black landscape. It works every time. You feel the wind through your hair. Out in the distance, far away.

The party is stateless. No place for Holland, England, France or Italy here. No place for nationalism. They're gone at long, long last. Those excruciatingly tedious exhibitions of seven—it always seems to have to be an odd number, doesn't it—Dutch artists in Reykjavik, or contemporary —because new is good—art from Germany. At the party, it's all about art. It's not that art has become so universal, it's far from that. It is about culture, time, colour and particular places. Hopefully people will discover that, sooner rather than later. Life's too short. Party poopers are more than willing to crash our party. Academics, Calvinists, fingers wagging, declaring our party ridiculous, vulgar, obscene and taboo. They will bring back Granny's kitchen, declaring it all right and proper. We haven't even got Calvin out of our system yet. That'll be the transition. But, hey, at least we're working on it.

9.15
THE CASE

Carefully she crept up to the top of the dune and peeked through the marram.
Nothing? No wait, when she stretched her neck, she could see the trespassers.
There were two of them. But what on earth were they doing there?
They weren't exactly sunbathing, were they?

9.17
DEPRESSION

The only thing Peter could do, was stare at her with eyes like saucers. Was she really planning to do what he thought she was? Here? In this absolutely packed restaurant?

LA SCALA

S.

Garden. Sweet smells. Serving tray.

"You're the best thing that ever happened to me."
"Where have I heard that one before?"
"It sounds like you're trying to chat me up.
Though it's not as if there's any competition
around here."
"Let me look at you, admire you, caress you."
"All right, enough already. Relax."
"For us there's no time, no yesterday,
no tomorrow."
"Excuse me?"
"Uhm..., huh..., erm..., well I'm trembling."
"Maybe we should go back to work?"
"No! Let me get this off my chest
—once and for all."
"Waiter, same again please."
"I don't know, it's all so sudden, so confusing."
"Let me tell you a secret—I wouldn't trade you
for anything in the world."
"Now, that's a real secret."
"Words cannot describe how much
I'm enjoying myself."
"Where are we going for dinner?"
"My spirit is overcome by beauty."
"Aren't you jealous?"
"Absolutely not—I've just got a vague sensation
of anxiety in my stomach."
"Things are going all right, aren't they?"
"So I've heard, but who knows?"
"You're not getting all paranoid, are you?"
"I think it's wonderful and all so clear."
"Beauty is highly seductive, but it can
paralyse you."
"Aren't you getting a little carried away?"
"It leads to absolute ecstasy and sweet
melancholy."
"To death as well."
"Oh stop it, you've been going on about
that for years."
"It's not as if I'm the only one."
"They've been going on about everything
for years."
"That's what they say, but who are they."
"Le temps gagne toujours."

H.

Bridge. Hot and dusty. Chair.

"Of course, time conquers all."

"Keep it moving, that's the answer."

"Explanation please."

"To start with, you need plenty of different interests. You can always focus later. If you try it the other way round, it all gets so incestuous."

"Doesn't it get confusing, so many choices?"

"Rest assured, someone who can cook a delicious five-course dinner will never be short of friends."

"Are you trying to say that quality is the only thing that counts?"

"Well, you need attitude to achieve quality."

"On the face of it there's not much similarity between your works, is there?"

"Look at those magnificent galloping horses."

"Similarity is vital for the recognition of the unknown."

"You're implying the unknown needs repetition?"

"Repetition contradicts the principle that art should reveal the unknown."

"However, for art to be accepted repetition is necessary."

"Now, there's a paradox for you."

"But a nice clear statement."

"No..., more like a sob-story."

"Someone said an idea is not the same thing as a perception. What do you think?"

"Art destroys itself time and again. Maybe that's why it is still around."

"Fire wrapped in paper?"

"And who's responsible for that?"

"Le postillon d'amour."

E.

Highway. Morning mist. Static on the radio.

"What an enviable messenger."

"Congested roads."

"I'm afraid I don't know very much: what does this thing of yours mean?"

"What sort of stuff do you do?"

"People often ask me that. It stems from an old belief that things should have meaning."

"But if nothing means anything, can there still be a something?"

"Once you see something, it's there."

"You're ignoring the laws of human nature —always wanting to understand what you see?"

"Yeah, you're right. Your question is perfectly valid and shows the incapability of depicting something different."

"What are you talking about?"

"Of course, with hindsight the principle is clear and completely acceptable."

"The problem is, I really don't understand what you are saying. If you cross the street chances are there's always someone who will say something."

"Hang on, the mist is getting thicker, I can barely see a thing."

"When I can't see anything my eye tries to compensate and I see something in nothing."

"All ways of looking are limited and yet always stay in the mind."

"Yeah, isn't that great?"

"What about your own taste? How can you get beyond it?"

"I've never felt the need to go beyond anything."

"But things are never nothing."

"Yes, but I've no say in that. The only thing I sometimes have doubts about is expertise."

"Finally you get it!"

"You can identify expertise, but that doesn't really tell you anything."

"It's just a retreat, back into convention. And ensuring you don't wash your dirty laundry in public."

"On the contrary."

"La chair est triste, hélas! Et j'ai lu tous les livres."

,.

Night. Mildew. Damp.

"I've read these books already."
"But they're all classics."
"It seems so superficial to pass judgements
like that."
"Could we have culture without judgements?"
"Judgements are all around, but are they
culturally important?"
"That sounds like a contradiction."
"Sure, it's the judgement that counts,
not the person."
"The idea of the individual has long since
vanished from our culture, even if people pretend
such a notion still exists."
"So who is going to stand up and speak? Is there
any scope for criticism?"
"Critics play all sorts of tricks when it comes to
defending themselves. Usually they get no further
than descriptions or irrelevant judgements."
"What's the point of having them?"
"Without them, life would be a lot duller."
"And we wouldn't have as much to read."
"We're surrounded by a veil of words."
"What? Like this?"
"It's basically the same, but it doesn't
mean anything."
"Aren't you mystifying this a bit?"
"Do you like the *petits fours*?"
"What about this?"
"Of course everything that is not immediately
understood could be called alienating. Otherwise
you slide down the slippery slope of didactics."
"Surely things aren't so black and white?"
"Of course, please forgive me, I was getting a
little carried away."
"Are you looking for the definitive statement?
Searching for a hero?"
"The thing I like about statements is that they
always satisfy the need for theory without having
to read hefty books—without pictures."
"They seem so indestructible, yet at best they're
just the appendix to a dictionary."
"The sky is blue, your eyes are shining."
"Exactly."
"Si tu veux nous nous aimerons avec tes lèvres
sans le dire."

S.

Beach house. Cocktails. Three little dogs.

"Let's make love without words."
"I'd like nothing better."
"Would the work speak so eloquently
without you?"
"Undoubtedly. You'd start looking for a substitute
immediately."
"But your presence and advice are so valuable."
"Thanks a lot."
"It's so quiet, isn't it."
"Why? What makes me so indispensable?"
"The simple fact that you're here and have
a name."
"But?"

"I control everything around me, but it's all in aid
of my chosen ideal."
"I don't follow you. You've already said that
looking for the ideal is pointless."
"Okay, you have a point. The ideal is a paradox.
Theoretically speaking you could reject it, but
there is an irrational urge to achieve something."
"If that's true, there must be an ideal and
therefore things can develop."
"That's right, but it depends on the ideal."
"And that could be?"
"Oh, moving comes pretty close."
"An ideal without a goal, without a higher
calling?"
"That's clever. You see, without you I'm nothing."
"Cool but not refreshing."
"Every moment, every emotion, every place,
they're all responsible for the way you move,
even I."
"I know. I just don't see myself as an individual.
I'm the creation of my environment, maybe even
the creator."
"You receive, select and reflect
—an ancient principle."
"Perhaps."
"Rien n'aura lieu que le lieu."

O.
Setting sun. Rope. French 'péniche'.

"Nothing's happening."

"I enjoyed last night, how about you?"

"On nights like that I always feel as if I'm travelling back in time."

"Isn't that nice?"

"Not as nice as it used to be. The atmosphere is so much more exciting than the action."

"Can't you ignore it?"

"Yeah, mostly, but only out of courtesy, by just accepting things the way they are."

"But what if you get so excited that you can't sit still."

"Of course, you get my point. And yet it still seems to be nostalgic *décor*."

"An odd repetition, the atmosphere as *décor*."

"The result is that everywhere is *décor*."

"And already defined by culture."

"Yeah, now I look at it that green is not bad at all."

"Is there anything else you want to mention?"

"Well, erm, I guess not."

"Although.... What's the problem with things just being gorgeous *décor*?"

"A theatrical festival complete with bells and whistles."

"Shaken up out of our lazy cultural habits."

"A succulent idea, almost erotic."

"It's coming to me now."

"But this isn't the first time it's been tried, and it's always failed in the past."

"What's the problem with that. The fact that it happens at all is interesting in itself."

"And everything has been said about it?"

"One can never say enough."

"Look, the curtain's moving."

"Getting a little excited aren't we?"

"Anticipation."

"This looks pretty good, doesn't it?"

"Too good, too good to be true, but what the hell."

"It's the heat of the moment that dictates the success of the *décor* and the *mise-en-scène*."

"Just like the real thing."

"Don't be such a cynic. It's not appearances that count, but the drama in the mind."

"Le temps gagne toujours."

THE BOU INANIYE MEDERSA IN FEZ
THE GARDENS OF UJAN AND SHAM IN TABRIZ

THE BAGH-I FIN IN KASHAN
THE GENERALIFE IN GRANADA
THE SHALAMAR BAGH IN LAHORE
THE GARDEN OF THE BULKAWARA PALACE IN SAMARRA
THE IMARAT-I KHUSRAW IN QASR-I SHIRIN
THE MADÏNAT AL-ZAHRÃ IN CORDOBA
THE SHAH GUL IN TABRIZ

THE JAWSAQ AL-KHAQANI IN SAMARRA
THE REVAN KIOSK TOPKAPI IN CONSTANTINOPLE

15.3
FOREST OF FONTAINEBLAU, SEINE-ET-MARNE

Let the enemy think. Worry. Wonder. Uncertainty is the most chilling thing of all.

3.32
VITRY-SUR-SEINE

The mass of the matter, that appeared at both electrodes as a result of the electrolytical process, is directly related to the power of the electric current and the length of time.

1	2	3	4	5	6	7	8	9
2	4	6	8	1	3	5	7	9
3	6	9	3	6	9	3	6	9
4	8	3	7	2	6	1	5	9
5	1	6	2	7	3	8	4	9
6	3	9	6	3	9	6	3	9
7	5	3	1	8	6	4	2	9
8	7	6	5	4	3	2	1	9
9	9	9	9	9	9	9	9	9

1

LES PRIVILÈGES DE LA PROMENADE
II

I REMEMBER THE WAY TO GRANADA, a city north-west of the Sierra
Nevada desert. The city nestles amongst the hills. There is only one road
that leads to the hill where the Moorish palace, the Alhambra, was built.
Most people come to visit the palace, but I am mainly interested in visiting
the Generalife, the garden of gardens. Finally, I will experience this bastion
of Vedic principles in the flesh.

Every form we know and everything we build is rooted in Vedic mathematics.
It originated in northern India and Persia and was then adopted and
developed by the Arabs. It enabled them to be the first builders of large
and complex vaulted structures. In contrast to our modern understanding,
Vedic mathematics depends on the inventiveness of the mathematician.
The higher his creative insight, the more he is accorded respect.

The basis of this understanding is a simple square, the Vedic square. The
Arabs didn't work with numbers higher than 10. The simple calculation of 8
plus 7 didn't add up to 15 but to 6, adding up the first and second digit of the
first sum. By using Vedic squares and by linking different, though related
numbers, it is possible to create patterns that we recognise as typically Arabic.
These patterns are the basis for the construction and decoration of almost
every Arabic building, from tilework to plastering and ceiling decoration.

I find it amazing that this mathematics, which appears to have been used
by Albert Einstein in his discovery of the theory of relativity, isn't applied
more often. All the more so as it fits so well with today's digital developments.
However, ask any mathematician about Vedic mathematics and he will
stare at you like a stuck pig.

Not only was the Generalife built according to Vedic principles, it soon
became a research centre for mathematicians—something which superceded
the Alhambra's role as a political centre.

Fortunately there are two separate entrances and I don't have to go through
the palace first. Within a few metres you realise there is no comparison
between the Generalife and the English or Renaissance gardens we know.
Examples like Le Clos Normand in Giverny, the Villa Farnese in
Caprarola, or Sissinghurst Castle Gardens are all built as additions to
existing architecture, conceived to enliven the building, to enhance its
status or to embellish its position within the landscape.

The Generalife was built independently from the Alhambra. The palace
was added later and built following the Moorish principles of the garden.

1	2	3	4	5	6	7	8	9
2	4	6	8	1	3	5	7	9
3	6	9	3	6	9	3	6	9
4	8	3	7	2	6	1	5	9
5	1	6	2	7	3	8	4	9
6	3	9	6	3	9	6	3	9
7	5	3	1	8	6	4	2	9
8	7	6	5	4	3	2	1	9
9	9	9	9	9	9	9	9	9

2

1	2	3	4	5	6	7	8	9
2	4	6	8	1	3	5	7	9
3	6	9	3	6	9	3	6	9
4	8	3	7	2	6	1	5	9
5	1	6	2	7	3	8	4	9
6	3	9	6	3	9	6	3	9
7	5	3	1	8	6	4	2	9
8	7	6	5	4	3	2	1	9
9	9	9	9	9	9	9	9	9

3

This influence is still reflected in the small square plaster patterns you can find in every room of the palace. Each one reveals a plan of a part of the garden that is then mirrored in the architecture of the room itself.

The Alhambra, or red palace—so called because of the red brick that was used for its exterior—comes across as a brutal, square fort. There is nothing to indicate the refinement inside. The same goes for the Generalife, which also conceals its treasures from the outside. Despite its age, it appears that the Generalife is well preserved. The main entrance is a long, narrow, slightly sloped lane of soft cypress trees, planted so closely together that they now form a soft dark green wall. The trees to the right have more distance between them, allowing a glimpse of the seedbeds, fish ponds, compost heaps and outhouses. No European garden architect would ever dream of locating the gardeners' sheds or compost heaps near the entrance of a garden.

The lane stops after more or less 100 metres. To both left and right are squares of flat stones through which trees and bushes grow. The view looks more like the ruins of an old architectural monument than a beautiful garden, covered in trees that have forced themselves through the piles of stone. There follows an amphitheatre built from narrow, red, partly overlapping stones. Some Italian gardens have theatres as well, but these are always separated from the rest of the garden by high hedges and often marble sculptures. Here the stage set consists of red stones, stairs, podia and the occasional cypress tree in the background. Because the trees are spaced

1	2	3	4	5	6	7	8	9
2	4	6	8	1	3	5	7	9
3	6	9	3	6	9	3	6	9
4	8	3	7	2	6	1	5	9
5	1	6	2	7	3	8	4	9
6	3	9	6	3	9	6	3	9
7	5	3	1	8	6	4	2	9
8	7	6	5	4	3	2	1	9
9	9	9	9	9	9	9	9	9

1	2	3	4	5	6	7	8	9
2	4	6	8	1	3	5	7	9
3	6	9	3	6	9	3	6	9
4	8	3	7	2	6	1	5	9
5	1	6	2	7	3	8	4	9
6	3	9	6	3	9	6	3	9
7	5	3	1	8	6	4	2	9
8	7	6	5	4	3	2	1	9
9	9	9	9	9	9	9	9	9

4   5

widely enough, you get the impression that the scenery behind them will be part of the stage set for an actual performance.

I'm starting to get excited.

Another square that also belongs to the theatre leads to the 'real' garden. A final flight of steps and then to my left and right the smoothest hedges I've ever seen. They feel like velvet, their colour a soft green. More than 1.5 metres wide and 6 metres high, these hedges are the green walls that divide the garden into its many different rooms. Here and there are small corners where you can sit down, elsewhere passages lead to other rooms. Low, neatly cut box hedges cover the floors with complex mathematical patterns. The squares are filled with perennials, the colours of which contrast with the greenery. Sometimes double hedges make up corridors. Every room is different. The Patio de la Acequia, for instance, is a long room in which water attracts all the attention. Its floor is an extended narrow irrigation channel with inward facing fountains over its entire length and flower beds along its borders. At the end of the garden is the Madïnat al-Zahrã. On every floor of this high tower there is a small pavilion from where you can look out over the entire garden, as well as get a panoramic view of the region. Then you discover the Generalife is built on a series of terraces high on the hill. It's like being on a roof garden. Looking down from the Madïnat al-Zahrã, for the first time you have a view on the overall structure of the garden. You understand why it doesn't really make sense to

1	2	3	4	5	6	7	8	9
2	4	6	8	1	3	5	7	9
3	6	9	3	6	9	3	6	9
4	8	3	7	2	6	1	5	9
5	1	6	2	7	3	8	4	9
6	3	9	6	3	9	6	3	9
7	5	3	1	8	6	4	2	9
8	7	6	5	4	3	2	1	9
9	9	9	9	9	9	9	9	9

6

1	2	3	4	5	6	7	8	9
2	4	6	8	1	3	5	7	9
3	6	9	3	6	9	3	6	9
4	8	3	7	2	6	1	5	9
5	1	6	2	7	3	8	4	9
6	3	9	6	3	9	6	3	9
7	5	3	1	8	6	4	2	9
8	7	6	5	4	3	2	1	9
9	9	9	9	9	9	9	9	9

7

talk about a 'garden'. I'd rather call it green architecture. Stretching out, in front of you, is a green palace without a roof, divided by living walls. Breathtaking.

Water flows and jumps, disappears and emerges somewhere lower down, sometimes swirling, sometimes tranquil. The subtlety of running and stagnant water has the same architectonic power as the green cypress hedges. In some ponds, the water is almost level with the edge of the tile floor that surrounds it. Again there is a correspondence between these patterns and the basic Vedic square. The fountains work on the principle of water pressure, using the natural water flowing down from the top of the hill. The perfection of the water channel system is such that seventeen fountains release exactly the same amount of water simultaneously.

The Escalere de las Cascades is one of the strangest constructions of the Generalife. A wide staircase, completely covered in sweet smelling plants, reaches a small pavilion on top of a hill, the former residence of the harem's leading lady. The balustrades of the staircase are hollow, allowing abundant amounts of fresh water to run through them. The sound of cascading water combined with the sweet smell turns this part of the garden into a beautiful, almost erotic experience.

It is said that in the Generalife heaven and earth meet. I don't know whether I agree with that. For me the Generalife is a roofless palace, an observatory, a planetarium and laboratory—not just a beautiful garden.

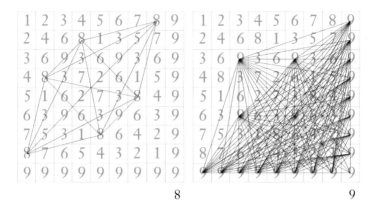

8   9

Beautiful gardens are everywhere, the ultimate form of decoration and beauty. They depend on the taste of their designers and the gardeners who maintain them. In the Generalife beauty is a result, not an intention. I consider it an elaborate, architectural Vedic monument.

The many different levels create a multitude of hidden and secret places. Three-quarters of the garden is secret. The surprise is that you never see the view you expect. Time and again the outlook is veiled by new, inward facing views, new insights. The beauty here is that this garden was the model for the Alhambra instead of the other way round.
The flowers are less important than in a typical garden, it is their smell —rather than their shape or colour—that is significant.

The Generalife is in a league of its own, easily comparable to other wonders of the world like the Pyramids of Gizeh in Egypt, the Nara Temple in Japan, the tombs at Angkor Wat in Cambodia or the Maharani Palace in Udaipur.

9.8
IMAGE OF AN ERA

Peter had great difficulties restraining himself. Looking around nervously, he was convinced everyone could see what was happening.

9.22
SABOTAGE

I do hope I haven't embarrassed you, she said, softly. You always seemed so tense, and
I thought that this would loosen you up a bit.

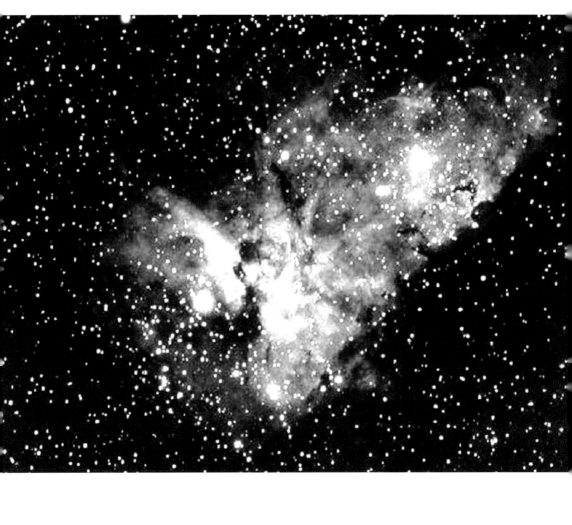

NO

You will find many stone stairways in the Jaipur observatory, each leading to an observation post. Each post is a window to a world.
Roaming from step to step you never feel that you're missing something. They carry you along.
A place like this is not about power, politics or the camouflage of mediocrity. Subtlety rules. Magnitude, sometimes a cheap attempt at invoking the illusion of power, that is often no more than an empty bubble, is absent here.

The year is 1988. Calgary. The most advanced techniques, the best materials, aerodynamic.
Intensive, scientific training—the performance, 1.09.14 seconds, 0.04 seconds behind comes number two. The only thing beyond measure is the tension —the pressure that comes from the fact that everyone is looking.
Perhaps this last obstacle will be gone by 1996. Other than that, nothing is left to chance, everything is under control—superficially at least.
Everyone knows the rules but ignores them nonetheless. So long as there are enough digits after the decimal point, there will always be a winner.

My name is Ramon and I had just turned eight years old when this picture was taken. Apparently it has a life of its own, a lot has been written about it. To my right is my twin brother. I remember the photographer took us to Madurodam. It was great—I felt like a lord and master. I could put my hand on the top of a cathedral and in one step I could cross the Westerschelde.
It was the first time that I was bigger than the world and I was one with everything around me.

S

A perte de vue, 1988
Acte de présence, 1987
Arcadia, 1985
Au fond du filigrane, 1987

H

Behind borrowed scenery, 1995
Behind the façade of analytical order, 1989
Box for something called art, 1996
But then again: a space is a space, 1985

E

Cataract, 1987
Catharsis, 1984
Closed Circuits, 1989
Coimbra, 1992
Comparable moments, 1988
Contient, 1994
Copyright, 1987
Coup de Foudre (Hommage aan R.), 1988

'

Datavault, 1991
De tweede loge links van Cygnus, 1984
Deuce, 1987
Do artworks have a sex?, 1990
Doublure, 1990

S

Echo, or the Fall of the Grand Tour, 1987
Either or, 1986
Éloge du regard, 1985
Entr'acte, 1989
Entre deux boîtes qui sont des maisons, 1992
Esplanade, 1994

S

Faux jour, 1989
Folie à deux, 1984

N

The battle of San Romano, 1982
The birth of Venus, 1982
The kiss of life (Resurrection), 1983
The narrow line between sight and seeing, 1986
The weight of folly, 1986
Trespassers will be executed, 1996
Tropic of Gemini, 1987

D

Untitled, 1982

A

Veiled deceit, 1991
Venus Fly Fall, 1983

S

Waar is dat eiland waar slechts huizen staan?, 1983
We never said goodbye to each other, 1983
*Where did you sleep last night that this morning you came home brushing
dewdrops?, 1995*

T

Zonder titel (Palazzo Sagredo), 1988